# People and Spaces

# People and Spaces

## A View of History Through Architecture

# by Anita Abramovitz

## Illustrated by Susannah Kelly

The Viking Press
New York

First Edition
Text Copyright © Anita Abramovitz, 1979
Illustrations Copyright © Susannah Kelly, 1979
All rights reserved
First published in 1979 by The Viking Press
625 Madison Avenue, New York, N.Y. 10022
Published simultaneously in Canada by
Penguin Books Canada Limited
Printed in U.S.A.
1   2   3   4   5   83   82   81   80   79

Grateful acknowledgment is made to Gambit and
John Murray (Publishers) Ltd. for permission to
quote from *Sailing to Byzantium* by Osbert Lancaster.

Library of Congress Cataloging in Publication Data
Abramovitz, Anita. People and spaces.
1.  Architecture and history.    2.  Architecture and
society.    I.  Kelly, Susannah.    II.  Title.
NA2543.H55A27     701     78-24555     ISBN 0-670-54705-0

To Max

Who taught me to see

# Contents

# People and Spaces

# Introduction

We shape our buildings. But why? And why the fantastic stream of varied shapes, sizes, and forms flashing through time and space from ancient civilizations, other societies and lands, to our own times and the structures we see around us?

Are there reasons why a Greek temple differs from an Egyptian temple? How did the church, the synagogue, the mosque come to be built as they are? Why a hacienda in one place, a saltbox in another? What is the meaning of a ziggurat, a pyramid, a cathedral? Why columns, arches, domes, balconies, arcades, windows, fireplaces, stairs, elevators, flat roofs, peaked roofs, courtyards, skyscrapers, ramps?

How did it all happen? What did we inherit, and what

have we invented? Can we recognize in the shapes of our rooms elements that come from early primitive eras, from the ancient Egyptians and the ancient Greeks? Can we see in our sports centers the ancient Roman arenas? Or in the courtrooms and churches of today the basilicas of yesterday? Are our shopping centers outgrowths with old roots in Greek agoras or Roman forums or ancient Arabian souks? Most important of all, what do these relationships mean? What, if anything, do they tell us about ourselves and history?

It is said that architecture lives in three-dimensional space — "lives" because that space, designed and built by human beings, also includes human beings themselves

3

—their comings and goings, their actual *presence* — throughout time and in ever-changing patterns. We ourselves, therefore, are the quality peculiar and unique to architecture, the dimension that distinguishes architecture from all other arts. It is we who call forth the kinds of spaces we need, desire, and enjoy. It is we who by our actions become part of buildings, moving about, around, and inside them.

Buildings taken over-all are an expression of the conglomerate lives of millions of peoples, present and past; an expression of society now and societies long since disappeared. Just as our gestures are parts of ourselves and our personalities, so the architecture of the past can be seen as the gesture of a whole society, a society whose personality we can try to reconstruct. Our ancestors influenced the architecture of their times, just as we, in our daily lives without quite realizing it, are constantly influencing the architecture of today and leaving a heritage for the future.

This book about spaces and people is also a book with a view of history, the European heritage; a book that attempts to understand the huge hieroglyphics that different peoples of the Western world have left behind. The emphasis in this book is on public buildings rather than private houses, because public buildings withstand the ravages of time better than most private buildings and are therefore more accessible to study for their relationship to a particular culture. They also reveal the general trends, the combined living of all people, rather than the idiosyncrasies of private living. When houses are discussed they represent typical examples which relate in some way to climate, technology, or type of civilization.

This is not a book about architectural styles except as they fit a trend, nor is it about particular architects, although architects and their abilities are everywhere between the lines. They are the crucibles from which come, in varying degrees of competence and talent, the expressions of the ages in which they lived. The answers to the "whys" of certain kinds of buildings cannot be found solely on the architect's drawing board, or in the engineer's office, or in the builder's blueprints. These men, too, belong to their times. However great their skill, they can only articulate and sometimes anticipate the kinds of shapes and spaces their society needs and wants.

The architect has not always been known in the professional sense we know him today, and his training, status, and social standing varied throughout the centuries according to the values of the civilization of which he was a part. In Egypt, for example, he was usually of the priest class, highly esteemed and often among the most important personages of the time. In Greece and also in fifteenth-century Europe, the time of the Renaissance, he was almost always a sculptor and skilled craftsman as well as a planner and builder. In medieval Europe, a period during which the early Christian Church became the most prolific builder, the architect was a layman expected to have technical knowledge but was considered lacking in knowledge of theology and therefore without distinction or much social status. It was during the Renaissance that the word "architect" began to denote a version of the modern trained professional.

When we speak of architects or architecture—which has an awesome number of definitions, ranging from the somber scientific of the dictionary to the poetic "frozen music"—we are using the terms in their most general sense. We are not interested here so much in an analysis of what is "meant" by architecture as we are in ways of looking at buildings in order to understand our present environment, as well as that of the past.

A building standing empty is not a whole building. It is only a beginning. We cannot understand it until we fill it with people, if only in our imaginations.          A.A.

# Seeing Forms and Spaces

I n order to understand a building — any building — it is important to be able to *see* its spaces, and the key to seeing space is to experience the three-dimensional void between forms, the content, which architects call the *volume*. In the case of a simple room, the walls, the floor, and the ceiling would define the void; in the case of a courtyard, the walls and the ground; in the case of a steeple or a dome, the space inside the form.

In general, when we look at an object, we can say we saw it from the front, the back, or the side, near or far. When we are in a room, we usually are aware of details of lines, colors, or

6

*Stonehenge (England): A mysterious encirclement of space*

sizes, and two dimensions — a tabletop, a chair back or seat, a row of books, a rug — and are only half aware of all the three-dimensional forms there are and of how they break up the surrounding space.

We often look *at* and remember buildings in the same way. Perhaps this is because we are more accustomed to viewing facades or blueprints or miniature models empty of human activity, or to partial views of architecture given in photographs, than we are to seeing the three-dimensional spaces we move through. Yet to think of a building as merely floor plan is to liken the sea to a navigator's chart.

7

If we concentrate on recognizing three-dimensional forms in space, which is what painters, sculptors, and architects see, we will, in turn, begin to be aware of the spaces that surround us: They are closed in; why? They are complex, but we like them; why? They are complex, but we like them; why? They're peaceful, just right for a church; what gives us that feeling? They're dismal and dull; what would make them more exciting?

Architects talk about two kinds of space: *enclosed,* or interior space, and the unused, unfilled voids around forms, called *external* or, sometimes, *displaced* space. Enclosed space is the space we move about in, use for shelter, for living, for public business, for storage, and for worship. Displaced space gives us the shapes and characters of streets, towns, and cities; it is defined by the outer form of a building and the forms of the buildings around it. Every building creates and contains both kinds of space.

It is impossible to separate form and space; one creates the other. Consequently special connotations and characteristics of many geometric *forms,* acquired through long years of traditional usage, ethnic preferences, or sacred dictates, often influence the shapes, sizes, and arrangements of *spaces* in both ancient and modern buildings. Black Elk, a member of the Oglala Sioux, speaks of his house on a modern reservation:

> All our people are now settled down in square gray houses, scattered here and there across this hungry land, and around them the Wasichus (Americans) have drawn a line to keep them in. The nation's hoop is broken, and there is no center any longer for the flowering tree. It is a bad way to live, for there can be no power in a square.
>
> You have noticed that everything an Indian does is in a circle, and that is because the power of the world always works in a circle, and everything tries to be round. The sky is round, and I have heard that the earth

is round like a ball, and so are all the stars. The wind, in its greatest power, whirls. Birds make their nests in circles, for theirs is the same religion as ours. The sun comes forth and goes down again in a circle. The moon does the same, and they are both round. Even the seasons form a great circle in their changing, and always come back again to where they were. The life of a man is a circle from childhood, and so it is in everything where power moves. Our tepees were round like the nests of birds, and these were always set in a circle, the nation's hoop, a nest of many nests, where the Great Spirit meant for us to hatch our children.

But the Wasichus have put us in these square boxes. Our power is gone and we are dying, for the power is not in us any more.*

Shapes and spaces can provoke other kinds of responses as well. Some spaces seem appropriate to specific activities and expressions, and inappropriate or uncomfortable or even impossible for others. A person can *run* down a long hall, but must *climb* a rounded bell tower. Looking high into the space of a dome gives us a sense of calm and of the infinite, a very different feeling from the trapped sensation we get in a small, cell-like space with a low ceiling.

Geometric forms also have many different psychological meanings for us. The circle by its very nature — the continuity and endlessness of its line — is a most beloved form and has not only great symbolic significance but emotional and practical significance throughout architectural history.

It was a most efficient form for early mankind. It was easy to delineate. Ancient people stuck a stake in the ground, tied a string to it, pulled the string taut, and simply walked it around. The circle required the least amount of material to enclose space. A circular house was practical. A family or tribe could surround and benefit equally from fire, the

*Michael Freeman. "Ethnic Differences in the Ways that We Perceive and Use Space." *AIA Journal*, February 1977.

tribe's most precious possession, while a single hole in the rooftop easily (at least in theory) let out the smoke.

One can shift position in a circle, but one cannot escape the basic equality of the line. All those who surround the center are equally involved with it, whether that center is worship, argument, or an ancient magic ritual. Physically, a person cannot completely avoid another's eyes in the round; some of the hostility in direct confrontation is eliminated; and all who stand or sit in a circle, even though they may be in violent disagreement, still have taken a position on a connecting and infinite line, rather than a parallel or divergent one.

Special circumstances, however, sometimes call forth a very different individual response. When the redoubtable Sir Winston Churchill made a speech concerning the rebuilding of the House of Commons after World War II, he spoke passionately *against* a change to a circular chamber and *for* a continuation of the oblong or rectangular shape, because he recognized that there was political significance in the act of crossing the floor.

> There are two main characteristics of the House of Commons which will command the approval and the support of reflective and experienced Members. They will . . . sound odd to foreign ears. The first is a very potent factor in our political life . . . I am a convinced supporter of the party system in preference to the group system. . . . The party system is much favored by the oblong form. It is easy for an individual to move through those insensible graduations from Left to Right [in a circular assembly], but the *act of crossing the Floor* is one which requires serious consideration. I am well informed on this matter, for I have accomplished that difficult process, not only once but twice.*

*Sir Winston Churchill, October 28, 1943, in a speech to the House of Commons. Author's italics.

Churchill met with some opposition, but eventually he won his point, and the rebuilt House of Commons is a rectangular chamber today.

Frank Lloyd Wright, one of the great names in twentieth-century architecture, tells how, as a young child, he was strongly influenced by certain geometric forms that were used for play and design in the late 1870s. To Wright, the circle signified infinity, the square integrity, the triangle aspiration. If the square gives one a feeling of integrity, it may be because it conveys a sense of security, strength, and solidity. It was a form relatively simple to build. Its protective walls could be thickened to great depth, and its corners reinforced for strength and used for outlook posts.

It is the form we see in many fortresses, and in compounds and settlements that wish to be protected from the outside yet share an inside "commons." But the square has its limitations, too. It must stand as it is; it does not allow for expansion or variation. In various transitions, even our own slang remains steadfast to the basic solidarity of the square: to be on the square; to square off; to square something; to be a square. It was possible to build the square form in the earliest of times because a way was found to make a right angle using only pieces of string.

The rectangle is a much more flexible form than the square or the circle. It lends itself to variations and combinations, but it is therefore a trickier unit of space and was a more difficult geometric form for ancient man to learn how to cover or support. This was the challenge, and we see various solutions in buildings as different as the civilizations themselves.

Generally, the rectangular space proved to be the best for living, since it provided walls for benches, beds, cupboards, and furniture. It is a form that lends itself to gatherings and to the movement of many people within. We see it today in churches, schools, libraries, museums, many private houses, and all public buildings of general use.

The triangle is a form that has much to offer the mathematician, with its many possibilities for interesting angles and variable sides, but, for the architect, it is considered a rigid form because no angle can be changed without also changing the length of its sides. It therefore does not lend itself, except with a great deal of adjustment, to calm and easy interior space. It was used often by the ancients as an exterior form in pyramidal shapes for tomb monuments and shrines. We also see it tipping the obelisks, the slender monuments of the Egyptians; in many church spires; and in the nose cones of today's space rockets, where it pulls together other forms and points them toward the sky — the unknown.

The triangle form is a common sight in northern climes, forming the slopes of pitched roofs. Less obvious to the spectator but of great importance to builders, engineers, and architects, however, is the combination of triangles used *under* many roofs. Here the rigidity of the triangular form proved an asset with the invention of the *truss*.

The truss is the result of a construction principle of triangulation which came relatively late in technological progress in spite of the fact that early wandering tribes, in designing their tents, instinctively followed the general theory of distributing vertical weight from one point to many. The truss, or series of trusses, developed over the years has been one of the important techniques used by builders to roof over large areas with an economical use of material, and without requiring the support of heavy posts or columns, which would break up the space below. So the triangle can be said to have a profound effect on interior space, after all, and has made possible our large auditoriums, convention halls, and many vast station and airport areas.

Although two-dimensional names have been used here for

*An Egyptian obelisk, dedicated to the sun god, points to the sky.*

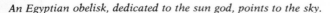

the simple geometric shapes, we see them and move through them in their third-dimensional forms, such as the sphere, the cube, the cone. Spaces know us well. They have seen millions of us come and go. But how well do we know them?

Our ways of living and thinking—our habits, needs, fears of enemies, aspirations, materialistic concerns, and religious beliefs—have influenced the kinds of spaces that we build and that later surround and include us *(people)*. But are we the only players in this particular historical drama? Or are there other factors which determine shape and form and, therefore, spaces?

Clearly, shelter in lands of constant, bright, hot sun differs from shelter in areas where rain, sleet, snow, and ice have long seasons. So *climate*, meaning the permanent condition as distinguished from local, changeable, everyday weather, is an obvious and important influence. Past climates are forever recorded in the window openings *(fenestration)* of a building. Their size, number, and style, their placement — toward or away from the sun, to the east, west, or north, whether arranged high or low, whether primarily for light or security — these are all clues to living conditions in a particular climate.

Roofs, too, are given their shapes and functions by climate — sloped or pitched for winter snows, tiled for insulation against the hot sun, or finished flat to serve as an extra room for some of the Mediterranean peoples and for the ancient Egyptians, who used them for sitting out in the cool of an evening.

Before a space could be enclosed to make a single room, a way had to be found to hold up walls and a roof, to provide openings to let in light (windows), and also of getting in and out (doors). Before several rooms, as we know them, could be built, ways had to be found to enclose and roof over several different spaces. Before the vaulted chambers of the

*A triangle in the form of a truss supports a wooden roof.*

great cathedrals could be built, it was necessary for someone to know not only how to make an arch but to be sure of
what it could support. So, *technology*, or the skills and
methods of building known to a civilization at any specific
time in history, has been a most important and often a
dramatic influence on the shapes, sizes, and characters of
buildings.

The *materials available* for building in the past are another
clue to the geography and economy of a region. What materials were indigenous? How far-reaching and expensive was
transportation, and how rich or poor was a civilization?
How close to the sea was it, and, as a result, what was it able
to bring from outside?

Many materials that we take for granted were unknown or
impossible to obtain in ancient civilizations, which existed
self-contained in pockets of time and space. Where there
were trees to be cut down, buildings were made of wood;
where there was stone, the stone of the region, whether
marble, limestone, granite, or any other variety, made the
public buildings; and where there was mud or clay, mud or
clay or sun-dried brick made the houses.

The influence of *economics*, which includes the availability of manpower and costs of materials as well as the
financing of construction, is closely linked to the culture of
an epoch and the varying social conditions, of, for example,
an ancient slave civilization, a priestly or royal hierarchy, or
a modern industrial society.

There are two more influences that have fundamental
effects on the character of all buildings. One is the proposed
use of the building to be erected. Architects call it the *purpose*. What kind of building is required — a house, a barn, a
church, a theater, a school, an office building, living space
for hundreds of people?

*Site*, like purpose, is a fixed, specific influence that deter-
mines the form and character of a building. Sites chosen in

the past give us clues to the economics of a civilization at the time of building, the availability of materials in that area, and the proposed use of the building. Often the beliefs or the apprehensions of people were a strong factor in choice of site, as in the building of temples or fortified cities. This explains many site choices in the Mesopotamian valley, in ancient Greece, and in the castle and city sites of the Middle Ages.

Throughout history these seven factors have always been present in different degrees and combinations and have combined with people's mores and religious beliefs to characterize buildings. Sometimes one factor will predominate, sometimes another; often several will overlap. All serve as *ever-present* controls and challenges for anyone who builds, including the architect.

# Shelter: In the Beginning

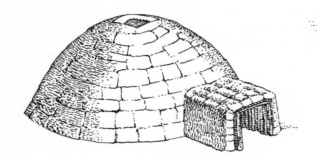

"I need that space for my use and comfort," says Man.

"You'll have to push me out, or change me," says Nature. "Be satisfied with my natural caves, trees, and overhangs."

"I'll work with and around you," says one kind of builder.

"I'm in a hurry," says another. "Move over or I'll level you."

"I'll rain on you," says Nature. "My suns will burn you."

"Then I'll build a covering, a roof."

"My trees and vines and foliage will overwhelm you; my wild beasts will hunt and destroy the animals you tame."

16

*Primitive dwellings*

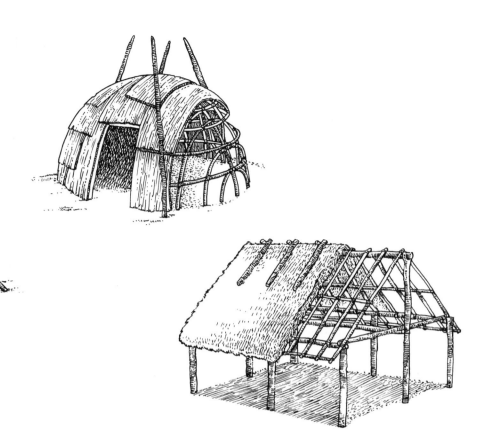

*"Then I'll build a wall," answers Man, "and behind it, a shelter for myself and my animals. . . ."*

A building or a space should make one feel that a thought is within it, that it is more than a shelter, just as a good book is more than words put together, or music is more than an arrangement of notes. Nevertheless, shelter continues to be a basic motivation for building and a characteristic of all buildings. What started as a primitive house to protect members of a tribe from the elements and, often, from their fellowmen, came to include a whole environment. Architecture as shelter became not only shelter for people but

17

for their animals and produce — barns, silos, and storehouses — and for their work — public buildings, factories — and for their gods and religious treasures and symbols — temples, churches, cathedrals. Museums shelter man's artistic and historical treasures; banks his coinage; tombs his spirit after death.

In the beginning man needed *two* things: shelter and protection. He needed shelter *from* the elements (*climate*) — storms, winds, heat, cold — and shelter *for* his great discovery — fire — and his most important possessions — his animals. He needed protection (*site*) from wild animals and thieves and enemies. He needed to be within reach of water (*site*).

To build, he needed *materials*, or the ingredients — water and earth — to make materials, or the bartering power to obtain them (*economics*). He needed some basic knowledge and skill (*technology*). He did not have the choices we have, but he had some, and he held beliefs and desires that qualified and influenced his choices (*people*). All these needs have developed but basically have not changed.

The safest arrangement for early man was to be protected at the back and to have the front clear for vision and movement. Consequently, when man moved out from natural caves, one of the first forms to be used by him was what we now call the *lean-to*.

Not all people built lean-tos, for even in the primitive world there were vast differences in climate and territory. Some early men dug dwellings out of the soil itself, living underground, with removable roofs and fields above. Some carved living space out of existing natural formations of stone or hills, or, in the frozen North, snow and ice. And somewhere, sometime during that long-ago age, an extraordinary breakthrough was made, and technology established itself firmly as an influence in the art of building. Someone thought to pile stone onto stone to build the first wall. Probably the walls were built originally for the purpose of retaining earth and water, but soon they became a basic part of one of man's earliest constructions for living — a circular hole in the ground surrounded by a low wall made of fieldstones, on top of which pine or other branches were used to form a tent-type roof.

Along with the breakthrough thought of piling stone on stone to make a wall, early man left us another basic construction idea, one that has lasted throughout all the centuries of building and can be seen in all styles of architecture. It is called the *post and lintel.*

When the primitive builder discovered that two upright stones would support a horizontal one, he tried it out with wood, and the timber hut was born. Posts were set in the ground, spaced apart and topped by connecting horizontal pieces (beams). The spaces between posts were filled with mud plastered over twigs and vines; in a hot climate woven

*An early example of post-and-lintel construction shows how size, weight, and the nature of the horizontal beam limited the amount of open space between the upright supports and influenced the nature and character of the posts or columns.*

grass matting was stretched between. The roofs were made sometimes of reeds, sometimes of clay. Householders were ingenious, too, with their roof styles. In certain parts of Nigeria roofs were made to be lifted in one piece off the walls, so that when the wall timbers rotted in the damp soil (*climate*) or the family had to move for other reasons (*people*), a roof could be moved bodily to top another house.

As for the post and lintel, we have gone on using it as a basic structural principle in larger buildings, in wood, or cut stone — marbles, granites — and, even later, in steel. We see the post and lintel in Greek temples, in our own doorways, in our houses, and in all buildings where straight walls — like posts — hold up the horizontal beams of floors and roofs.

The transition from the life of the wandering tribe to a settled existence was an important change in the history of mankind and also significant for architecture. In architecture shelter was no longer thought of as a purely private need but became a general concern, with public buildings and religious edifices. This was the beginning of that profound and never-ending influence of social customs and religious beliefs on public architectural forms and spaces.

For some early civilizations temples were centers for housing a special class of people more knowledgeable than the general public in the tenets of the local religion, or were citadels sheltering and guarding the artifacts of that religion. For others, temples were sanctuaries sheltering the spirit of a god, or a house for a god or several gods. Some temples were labored over with the aim of creating a magnificence to honor the gods, or to impress them as well as other societies. Religious buildings as meeting places for community worship did not come until much later, but in ancient times the religious complexes, or the areas around them, were also the centers for various nonreligious activities, including markets and law courts.

In the earliest civilizations the link between materials available and new technological advances was also a close one. It was an interdependence which, because of its challenges, encouraged creativity. Lack of certain materials, for example, was a challenge met by the development of techniques to use what was available, and these new techniques, in turn, encouraged builders to experiment with new forms.

The history of the brick is a good example, for the knowledge of how to make bricks eventually led to the development of the *arch and vault,* which, along with the post and lintel, and the truss, is one of the three great construction principles of all time. Just as the post and lintel had to come *before* the Greek temples could be conceived, so the principle of the *arch*, the *vault*, and the *dome* had to be discovered and developed before the design plans of the great Byzantine churches could be built or envisioned by architects.

Brick was the material of the Mesopotamian valley, a low-lying, marshy area containing almost no stone or wood. Since the post-and-lintel method of building requires materials of straight cut — such as wood, stone, or marble — capable of spanning horizontally fairly large dimensions, the early Asiatic builders had a formidable problem: how to build and roof over with the materials at hand. The problem greatly taxed their ingenuity, since the most abundant and easily procurable material was simply clay, and unfired clay itself cannot support weight.

Their solution was to compress the clay in molds, dry it in the sun, and make bricks. They now had small-size rectangular blocks. The next problem was how to hold them together to make them into a useful building material. At first they used mud to cement the bricks together. Later a new technique developed: bricks were made harder by baking in special ovens, and the clay was used also as mortar. In this way an indigenous material, clay, was used not only for filler and some walls, but turned into a new, strong material which was to characterize all the ancient temples and palaces of the Mesopotamian valley.

Thousands of bricks can make a wall, a floor, or a platform, but they do not make a building unless some principle is invented that can turn those small oblongs into support. And so, as the art of making, cementing, and decorating brick flourished and improved, so did the techniques of building.

The *arch* in its simpler forms was known to many ancient civilizations and to both the Egyptians and the Greeks. They used it sparingly, however, never developing its potential, since the stone and wood available to them were more than sufficient for post and lintel, which also satisfied their spatial and aesthetic needs.

The arch is at least six thousand years old. There is some question as to who invented it, if "invented" can be used to describe insights that reveal new structural possibilities. Some say that it was the Assyrians; some say it was the Sumerians who were the parents of the first arch forms that went further than the primitive, rudimentary affairs that resembled those carved out of rock. In any case, the development of the arch cannot be separated from the existence of the brick, because arch construction calls for materials of small size.

The arch shape must have been in the minds of primitive cultures, which saw it in nature's caves. They must have realized early that they could carve out replicas or at least widen and deepen openings. The next experimentations were probably with stones, piling them in attempts to meet at the top. This eventually led to what architects call *corbel* construction.

An old proverb says, "The arch never sleeps." This is because the thrust of the wedge-shaped stones, called voussoirs, is constant and is what holds and stabilizes the form.

Corbel construction is the same thing as *cantilever* construction. It is merely a bracket-type extension with one end built into a wall or fixed by some other means. The end projecting outward is then used to carry some kind of weight. Balconies are a good example, as is the round stone beehive hut, which is all corbeled construction.

The corbel arch shape was made by placing large, shaped stones one upon the other, each higher stone lighter than the one below and projecting slightly. Corbeling was used to make both arches and vaults, vaults being simply a con-

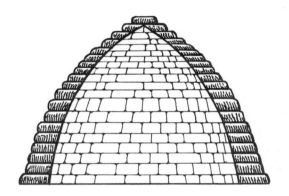

*Corbeling is a method of building by layering, in which the weight of each layer is balanced by the layer below. The beehive hut is an early example of corbeling; the corbel balcony is more decorative and led to the modern version of the corbel principle —the cantilever.*

1. Gothic
   *(Medieval)*
2. Etruscan
   *(Pre-Roman)*

3. Scalloped arch
   *(Islamic)*
4. Romanesque
   *(Twelfth century)*

5. Horseshoe
   *(Moorish)*
6. Foliated
   *(Late Gothic)*

*Every culture, even every era, has developed its own decorative variation of the arch form.*

tinuation of arch construction over a longer depth, forming a sort of tunnel. But the arch and vaults as we know them today had to wait for a further technical development called *centering*.

Centering is the building of a support, usually wooden, to hold wedge-shaped stones or bricks until the arch form is finished and can stand by itself. The temporary support is then removed, and the arch, because of its wedge shape, fights gravity; it will not collapse so long as its base is stable and does not spread. The ancients must have put back many falling stones, using wood pieces to prop up crumbling corbel-type arches until they had time to repair them, before it occurred to them that the wood used for temporary props could be made into a frame on which to lay a new, lighter-weight arch with more potential for varied uses.

Once the principles of the way the arch form worked against gravity and the techniques of centering were understood, the arch was on its way — rounded, pointed, scalloped, vaulted, domed — to become one of the great distinctive structural elements of architecture.

While post and lintel is what we see in most Egyptian and Greek architecture, we cannot look at a Roman building or a derivative of Roman style without seeing the arch or sensing it in the underlying structure. Roman builders and architects found the arch form much to their liking. They picked it up as an idea, puzzled over it, and found ingenious ways to use it instead of columns and beams for support. They played around with it in much the way a musician plays around with a basic theme. They tried it straight, in combinations, and finally with numerous variations. The Romans became virtuosos on the Theme of the Arch, and by their courageous and imaginative use of the form, they gave the world breakthroughs in structural knowledge, legacies that influenced all subsequent European architecture.

*Here wedge-shaped stones are being placed on a wooden centering form to make a high, rounded arch.*

# Stargazers and a Sun God

W hen we speak of ancient religious buildings, we are speaking of a type of structure that is usually the greatest, largest, latest, or finest of the kind that a society built for its use.

The ancient temples were built over a period of many lifetimes of people who individually and collectively lived through continuous changes. The boundaries of their civilizations wavered and staggered throughout thousands of years. The buildings of the past, just as the buildings of today, varied in their purity, competence, and impressiveness of design. But because they strove to meet the particular needs and ideals of their time, they reveal trends in

26

*Approach to the temple ruins at Luxor (1570-1200 B.C.)*

civilizations and characteristics that show obvious differences in cultures.

Three aspects of life in the Mesopotamian valley about the year 3000 B.C. relate uniquely to the lives and religion of the people of that ancient civilization; no other culture could have built in the same way. One aspect relates to the lack of wood (*materials available*), so that a new material had to be invented (the brick). One relates to *climate* and *site*. One relates to the people whose mythic religion involved many different nature gods; the moon god, Nanna; the stars and their constellations; and the planets.

Mesopotamia translates to Land of the Two Rivers (the                    27

Tigris and the Euphrates). It was there that many ancient civilizations had their beginnings, living above low-lying marshland. To avoid the dampness of the swamps and the swarms of summer insects (*climate, site*), they learned to use the humble brick to build vast platforms, some as high as fifty feet above ground.

The astrological nature of their religion led to continuing attempts to build temples. A strange building, of unusual height for the times, developed. It was called a *ziggurat* and resembled a high tower built in a series of terraces with a temple or sacrificial shrine at the top which was reached by flights of steps or by ramps. The terraced structure was placed within a forecourt and a walled inner court. The ziggurat complex usually provided living quarters for the priests, but the temple itself was accessible to the people, used for temple rituals, processions, offerings and sacrifices to the gods. The ziggurat was an integral part of the city, a symbolic center around which the palace of the king, the treasury, and other important civic buildings were built.

Ziggurats also functioned as observatories, because priests were also astrologers. They were expected, from the ziggurats' high vantage points, to study the stars, foretell the future, and interpret the will of the gods. Ziggurat means "holy mountain," and each ziggurat temple was dedicated to the god to whom the city supposedly belonged. This gave the people a sense of sacred and eternal permanence within the walled architectural complex.

Because of its unusual height, the ziggurat has been labeled "the skyscraper of the ancient world." But skyscrapers of today owe nothing to its construction. What we have inherited are the raised brick platforms on which the ziggurat stood, the courtyards, the flights of stairways, the idea of ramps, which in Egyptian hands became even more significant, the idea of a complex, many-spaced center for various uses, and the terraces which gave birth to the fa-

mous hanging gardens of Biblical report. (The Tower of
Babel is also thought to have been one of the later ziggurats,
magnificently adorned with colored glazed brick.)

If you had lived in the Mesopotamian valley about the
second millenium B.C., there would have been no lack of
ziggurats to contemplate, to climb, or to move about in,
including new ones being built and old ones being reno-
vated and added to. In circling *up* a Babylonian ziggurat,
you would feel yourself above a swampy plain, in a high
place where it would not seem so strange to see magic in the
stars or to search the heavens for wisdom. To arrive at a
shrine at the top, perhaps one dedicated to the moon god or
the water god or the storm god, you would have walked
ramps, or climbed long flights of stairs, through stages of
color, very significant to you if you were Babylonian. Each
stage — white, black, blue, yellow, silver, and gold — would
have been painted to represent a planet. You might take
offerings on your climb, but in certain periods of ancient
civilizations you would hope to be the priest or priestess
going to the top, and not the sacrifice.

The houses of ancient civilizations, like the public buildings, were as native to their geographical location as a tree
that will grow in Spain but not in Scandinavia. This was due
as much to *materials available* as to the usual hot-versus-
cold *climate* influences. For building the average house, *materials available* meant, more precisely, materials on hand.
These were usually of the earth or were natural products
growing nearby. This was particularly true in Egypt, for
example, a country rich in granite and sandstone. Both
materials were difficult and expensive to quarry and transport. Stone was fine for the gods and the Pharaohs, but for
the ordinary family, even the nobility, more modest, less
expensive materials were closer at hand: the earth and the
papyrus reed.

And so the houses of ancient Egypt were built of mud,

*The ziggurats of the Mesopotamian valley and the religion that influenced their forms have disappeared, leaving us with reconstructions and scenes that tease the imagination.*

used in varying degrees of sophisticated technology, from huts of wattle-and-daub plastered reeds to wall-enclosed houses of sun-dried brick.

Wattle and daub was a kind of basketwork woven of twigs or reeds, which were then daubed with clay. The roofs of such houses were usually of turf. Wattle and daub has a long history. It was used not only in ancient civilizations but also in medieval times in the construction of the homes of serfs, and later it was the method used for filling in the walls of the earliest Colonial houses in North America.

Papyrus, which was plentiful in Egypt in antiquity — though not today — had many uses, aside from its well-known use as a writing material in the form of scrolls. Papyrus was a strong and pliable reed; it was the basis of Egyptian sails and cloths, boats, and many houses as well. There probably was enough papyrus in an ancient house to make several shelves of scrolls; papyrus stalks bunched and bound together made the posts and sometimes were used for beams, along with trunks of palm trees.

The use of materials natural to a country gave the ancient cities and countryside a much more homogeneous and one-with-nature look than we are used to seeing today.

But in ancient Egypt as well as in all other ancient civilizations there was a vast difference between ordinary housing and public buildings because public buildings were usually an embodiment of religious beliefs. Thus the Egyptians put their energy, their creativity, their wealth, and their labor into the building of living quarters for powerful royalty or priests, and into the building of temples and royal tombs.

The massive style of the Egyptian temples was due, in part, to *materials available* and to the Egyptians' choice of technology. The Nile valley was rich in stone, and this provided the basic material for the temples, the tombs, and some monuments. It is obvious that in order to support the weight of a stone beam in post-and-lintel construction, the supports have to be relatively close together.

The Egyptians knew the principle of a rudimentary arch but never experimented with it to any contributing degree. They unquestionably preferred a post-and-lintel principle of construction. Whether this was entirely an aesthetic choice, whether the authoritarian nature of their society and their great reservoir of slave labor prompted the building of monumental forms, or whether the influence was the need for flat roofs — which we shall see was related to their religious rituals — we can only speculate. In any case, the columns one sees in Egyptian temples are made of heavy blocks of finished (shaped) stone, generally have a bold, solid look, as if capable of carrying great weights, and are usually set close together.

The Egyptians used stone in the same way with increasing authority and force during an unbroken period of more than two thousand years. During all that time there were no unusual innovations, only variations on the same building principles. Some outside influences were absorbed, but Egypt was a small, inwardly oriented country, and the Egyptians continued to build the same *kinds* of buildings. This kind of immutability is difficult to imagine today when we see all around us inheritances and influences of hundreds of styles and their variations, and when we find manifold original changes that are much more than just variations in very short periods of time.

Our traditional buildings barely have time to become traditional before they are replaced by the new and urgent. But we are a new and urgent people, and the Pharaonic people were solidly traditional. Theirs was a society of rigid hierarchies, of great social differences: prisoners (slaves), indentured servants, peasants, and a large, well-to-do, literate class of civil servants. The enormous reserves of manpower in this strict, almost static society enabled the

Egyptians to build and care for the great buildings, but by standing still, resistant to change, the society became, along with its buildings, archaic.

The Pyramids are probably the most renowned form of architecture of the Egyptians. Nineteenth-century excavations left no doubt that the Pyramids were architecture directly related to the religious beliefs of the people, particularly their confident faith in an afterlife. In the minds of the Egyptians, the chief Pyramids were built as an eternal abode for their Pharaoh, who was believed to be a god. The

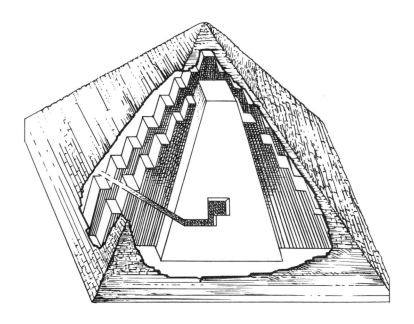

*An isometric section of a pyramid, showing a passageway to the innermost burial vault, the Pharaoh's chamber. The numbers and placement of chambers and air vents varied from pyramid to pyramid.*

pyramid was shelter as well as a monument. Seen in this context, it is not at all surprising that the Egyptian Pyramids contain chamber-like rooms surrounding the king's mummified body and are filled with treasures, possessions, household goods, even, in some cases, mummies of the king's family, his household, and persons of his court. And it seems appropriate that on the outside the Pyramids are great triangles which point to the sky and which command respect and awe.

But why that particular shape? There are many theories but no complete answers. Apparently, the impulse toward the pyramidal form came quite suddenly in Egypt, beginning with a stepped pyramid and attaining within a few decades the symmetry and volume of the great Pyramids of the Fourth Dynasty. But pyramid building in Egypt lasted only a few centuries, a brief interlude in the totality of Egypt's long history, and a short time, indeed, compared to the numbers of years Mesopotamian ziggurats continued to be built as religious symbols.

In the words of a modern architect, "Which other period of the past had the courage to tilt a triangle seven hundred feet long against another of equal length?"* The answer is that perhaps no other civilization of the time had the unusual mathematical knowledge, experience, and ability that developed in Egypt because of the nature of Egyptian society and because of its location. The Pyramids are an excellent illustration of how *site* and *societal* influences combined to create an ancient technological challenge.

All early civilizations were well-versed in techniques of irrigation. Water was, after all, their staff of life. In Egypt, it could be truly said, life depended on the flooding of the Nile. The flood made the difference between food and starvation

*Marcel Brewer in the Preface to *Living Architecture: Egyptian* by Jean-Louis de Cenival. New York: Grosset & Dunlap, Inc., 1964.

*The limited mechanical technology of the period required ingenuity and enormous reserves of manpower. Here, facing stones are being moved along earth ramps for the building of pyramids.*

for many Egyptians. The rise of the Nile had to be recorded and carefully studied, and there was a great need for carefully controlled irrigation in the fertile, flooding fields of the illiterate peasant farmers. There developed a class of engineers and administrators who were more educated than the peasant group. They also collected taxes, laid out plots, devised and supervised irrigation methods, settled land boundaries and other disputes, and managed royal property. These engineers and administrators had to be unusually competent in mathematics and elementary geometry, and it was their training that enabled the Egyptians to build a marvel of geometric form showing exceptional knowledge of gravity and weight, in a period when, as far as we know, the only known lifting devices were ramps, a method called rockers, and human muscle.

Since the enormously complicated Egyptian god-world

dominated Egyptian architecture for a period of almost three thousand years, it is well worth looking into this world in order to see the temples as something more than static masses in stone and to understand them as buildings that were a part of the life of the people.

Unless we throw our minds and imaginations back to four thousand years B.C., it may be difficult for us to understand the intensity of the *daily* meaning the gods and the Pharaoh had for the Egyptian of that time.

Although Egypt traded goods and often fought with its neighbors, it was, we must remember, a very small country. It was a wheat-producing strip of Nile valley not quite as big as West Virginia of today. But for the peasant who worked the land, who lived in a hut made of mud or sun-dried brick, it was the world. The land he tilled and his country were the peasant's lifetime framework. To such a person, who could not read, and for whom such things as the telephone or TV would have been some kind of inconceivable, frightening nightmare, the cycle of seasons, the mysteries of the night, the bounty of nature or its catastrophes — the rains, the floods, the intense heat of the sun — were all beyond his understanding.

So he created for himself a religion in which all things had a spirit, a religion full of daily manifestations of the gods. He believed in some kind of survival after death, and he held a true and absolute conviction that his king, the Pharaoh, the Pharaoh's ancestors and his next in line were themselves actual gods, as well as sons of gods. With a god in their midst, living among them as their ruler, godhood and god-family were concrete facts to the Egyptians, not an abstract idea. It seemed obvious to them that the well-being of one — the people — depended completely upon the well-being and goodwill of the other — the gods.

The gods, therefore, needed to be reassured constantly — actually needed to *see* demonstrated the fact that they were being worshiped, honored, and cared for in the best manner possible. Consequently, it was important that processions and rituals be carried out in impressive, suitable, and symbolic surroundings.

In any discussion of the religious beliefs of the ancient Egyptians, one must start with the king, the Pharaoh, for although ideas and images were bound to change somewhat over a period of three thousand years, in essence ancient Egyptian religion revolved around the presence of the king, living or dead. The Pharaoh was all; he was a god and son to the gods, of which there were many: Ra, the sun god, whose rays gave life to the world; Horus, the falcon god, one of whose eyes was the sun, the other the moon; Amon, a powerful deity also allied with the sun god and sometimes represented by a ram's head; and many others. For all these, theoretically, it was the Pharaoh, their son, who built the temples in which their statues were kept and cared for. The people were the workmen, the priests the maintainers of the rituals.

In viewing the temples, we must never forget that the Pharaoh was the unity and the power from which all flowed, as well as a living incarnation of *any* of the gods. The name Tutankhamen tells us this. It means simply, "living statue of Amon."

It was the duty of the priests to officiate at all rites, since the Pharaoh could not, of course, personally officiate throughout the country. However, the king's presence *was always there*. Carved on every temple wall were reliefs that show him carrying out his role.

There was also the statue of a chief god placed permanently in each temple. It was usually made of stone and of great height, so another smaller statue, made of wood or precious metal, was set in a small model of a boat so that it might be carried in processions.

Caring for a god's statue was the most important ritual

performed in the temples, which were built to shelter the god. Other rituals involved feeding and clothing the god's statue as well, and doing all those things that would encourage him to come to inhabit his statue so that he might be beseeched continuously to renew the workings of creation in order that the world (Egypt) would not fall back into chaos.

All the great deities had what has been called their solar character — that is, a relationship to the sun, giver of all light and energy. Thus, the god's statue had to be exposed to the sun, not only in public rites at great festivals, but daily in a secret religious ceremony. The statue was carried by a few privileged priests to a room with an opening to the sky, or up ramps onto a temple roof to be exposed to the rays of the sun and endowed with its divine energy. It was this ritual that made long ramps and flat roofs important characteristics of Egyptian temple buildings, and although these ancient rituals have no meaning in our modern society, flat roofs and long ramps still have a place in our architecture.

Light — that precious force idolized by the Egyptians — became, understandably, a chief concern of the temple architects. It was vital that it penetrate in the best possible way to the statue within the building; yet, since the nature of the god was unfathomable and obscure, there must remain around him shadows of mystery. This concern influenced the organization of all interior space in the temple in order that beams of outdoor light, in the manner of theatrical spotlights, might be made to fall into a room upon a statue otherwise in shadow. In time, also, Egyptian architects became masters not only of the directing of light, but of dramatic play with shadow, gradually increasing the darkness to suggest ever-deepening mystery. To create more mystery and to inspire awe, they combined light and shadow with related play of widening and narrowing inner and outer spaces following upon one another. To walk into

an Egyptian temple was to leave the hot, bright world outside and enter a mysterious forest of great painted and
carved columns, stretching back into an awesome dark infinity. You would move through shadow and light, surrounded on all sides by reliefs reminding you of your king-
god and the other gods. You would go from these spaces ever
inward through courtyards and shrines, through wide
spaces and narrow corridors, to silence and darkness,
lighted only by a ray of daylight pouring over a statue of a
god. This magic with light and shadow, with varied spaces
opening into each other, was one of Egypt's greatest contri-
butions to the aesthetics of architecture.

# Porticoes and Colonnades

F or the ancient Greek, as for the Egyptian, the public buildings, particularly the temples, were the focus of his architectural energies, but his beliefs, his whole approach to living, as well as his geographical situation, differed greatly from the Egyptian's. Therefore, so did his temples.

The Egyptians placated their gods, believing their destiny as a nation to be irrevocably tied to the well-being and approval of the god-families, but the Greek attitude was quite different. The Greeks, who also brought offerings to the gods, did so not so much because they wished to placate as because they were concerned about the gods' welfare. The

*An agora, or marketplace, in ancient Greece*

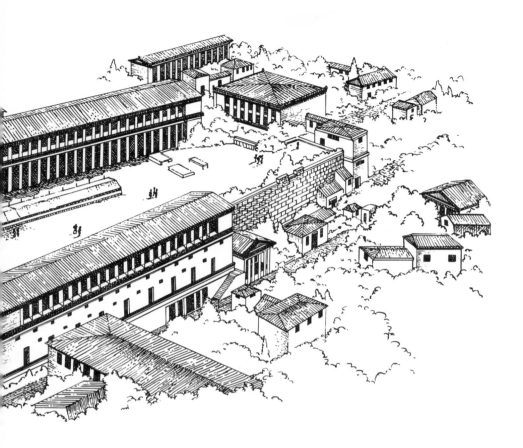

attachment between the ancient Greeks and their gods was a strong bond, and the gods' influence was felt in every aspect of life. According to the myths, the gods themselves carried on active lives of involvement and relationships with each other in a well-populated world of their own. The Greeks naturally expected the gods to understand human situations. They wanted the gods and goddesses to think of them as communities of individuals in need of protection, guidance, and counsel.

In the Greek's life there was no powerful class of priests, no all-powerful immortal god called Pharaoh. The Greek was, comparatively speaking, on his own. He participated in his community and in his government, and, in the same way, he and his neighbors took part personally in celebrations honoring gods and goddesses. His priests and priestesses came from the community. All this was a most important factor in determining the site and function of his temples, and in the development of the Greek theater and gymnasiums.

To look at a reconstruction of a classic Greek temple today is to see a dwelling place for a god or goddess. It is to see a rectangular space surrounded by rows of columns, called *colonnades*, which served as *porticoes* or porches.

The rectangular space is called a *cella* (or *naos*, meaning chamber). Architects refer to it as a closed space, a static, internal space never developed for active human use *because there was no reason to do so*. That space had no social function. The temple, looked upon by the Greeks as an impenetrable sanctuary for the god, was not planned for the caring for a god's statue, nor was it planned as a house of worship, as are the churches of today. Its interior spaces were purposely meant to shelter and to enclose mysteries. It was not a space for moving about in, for religious services, or for the conducting of State business (as the Romans later discovered).

Religious ceremonies in ancient Greece took place *around* the temple, so that the only spaces in the building in which most people moved or stood were the corridors of the surrounding colonnades.

The ancient climate, hot but clear, the sudden showers, the intense light were such that the Greeks, who loved the outdoors, carried on most of their activities, including the administration of justice, outside four walls. This proclivity for outdoor living was an all-important characteristic of ancient Greek civilization. It made the Greeks' society basically quite the opposite of ours and influenced their architecture in fundamental ways. As a result, modern-day im-

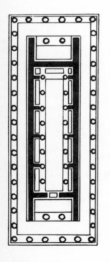

*A typical Greek temple floor plan. Interior spaces were influenced and shaped by religious beliefs.*

*Even a temple ruin (early fifth century B.C.) tells us the ancient Greeks achieved classic proportions and great beauty in buildings using post-and-lintel construction. Inner spaces (see floor plan, opposite) were sacred sanctuaries, not planned for public use.*

itations of their buildings, no matter how well designed, become copies of facades or of other single elements, but never achieve a sense of the original unified whole.

It is particularly important to see ancient Greek architecture in relationship to the environment of its time. Although we have inherited many separate architectural and philosophical elements from the ancient Greeks, none of the over-all physical and cultural environment has survived. Sometimes what we think of as Greek is only partly Greek, and thus distorted, in the same way that a statement taken out of context can distort meaning. Really to understand the ancient environment, we must first break through that curtain of enchantment with all things Greek that captivated all Renaissance thinking and that we have inherited.

Beginning about the sixteenth century, a kind of magic spell spread throughout most of the Western world, producing a rebirth that fascinated the humanists and scholars of the nineteenth century.

All aspects of ancient Greek civilization — politics, poetry, literature, drama, schools of philosophy, art, mathematical principles, and rules of order — were ardently researched, lovingly scrutinized, eagerly tested, and found worthy and good. As uncovered ruins revealed workmanship of great quality and near-perfect geometric form, it was generally agreed that the architecture of Greece was beyond doubt a model of elegance, simplicity, clarity, dignity, and grace. Probably no architecture of any civilization has been so admired, so passionately idealized, and so disastrously and impossibly copied. Yet the greatness of Greek architecture and the proof that it cannot truly be reproduced lie in the fact that it *was* such a completely unified and total expression of function and form *for the kind of culture it served*.

The phrases used by art historians, architectural critics, and architects to describe ancient Greek buildings sound overwhelming when we remember that these buildings were constructed almost twenty-five hundred years ago. Architects speak of geometrical perfection, perfect equilibrium, spiritual dignity, miracles of proportion, optical refinements, the kinship of form and function, matchless bas-reliefs, affinity with nature, and grasp of "human scale." All in all, they call the heritage from the Greeks one of order, harmony, and reason, expressed as a visible unity, and they gave the name "classical" to Greek architecture, which means having lasting significance or recognized worth.

Amazingly, it is all true. What, then, were the ancient Greeks like? Surely they must have been intellectual and mathematical geniuses, disciplined perfectionists! In our mind's eye, we begin to imagine a race of rare beings, idealized statues, silent, dignified, gliding in gown and toga through buildings of pure and perfect mathematical formulas, down endless corridors of finely wrought, fluted porticoes and colonnades.

Nothing could be further from the reality. And so we prefer three clue words of our own to explain the Greeks and their buildings. One is "outdoors," one is "scale," and the third is a word of their own, "paradox."

Paradox is defined as a tenet contrary to preconceived opinion; also as a person or thing exhibiting apparent contradictions. So, though their buildings were classic and calm and beautifully proportioned, the ancient Greeks as people were a lively bunch on the whole, lusty, seafaring, adventuresome, intensely human, energetic, and, above all, avid conversationalists.

Some Greeks were farmers, but the fertile areas were so limited compared to the Egyptians' Nile valley that a basic agrarian society could not have survived. Greece was linked to other peoples and other artisans by the sea. There were mountains, rich in marble — an ideal building stone. Greece was a nation of sailors, craftsmen, traders, and manufacturers. These vital characteristics, combined with the ancient Greeks' religious philosophy and their preference for the outdoors, were the chief determinants of a developing architecture. Greek architecture comes alive only when we people it with figures that walked, ran, and climbed, chatted, shouted, bargained, and argued — in fact, carried on almost all daily activity and entertainment *around* and *among* their public buildings rather than *inside* them. The market (*agora*) was open; a *stoa* was an extended colonnade, roofed over for the sudden showers and used as a promenade or meeting place; religious ceremonies, festivals, sacred games and ritual dances took place in sacred groves or on an acropolis. (*Acropolis,* meaning high+city, was the highest point and center of a city, usually the place where the sacred buildings stood for protection and dignity.) Entertainment, too, took place in open-air theaters, and another characteristic entertainment — the enjoyment of discussion and conversation — was carried on in the many porticoes and colonnades.

These porticoes and colonnades, so predominant in ancient Greek architecture, were not only fine places for long and casual conversations, but also afforded sufficient shelter from the hot sun and the sudden showers. We are told that the *Stoa Poecile* on the side of the agora of Athens was the favorite spot of the philosopher Zeno, whose followers were called *Stoics*, and their system *Stoicism* — much as if the New England farmers who sat around cracker barrels

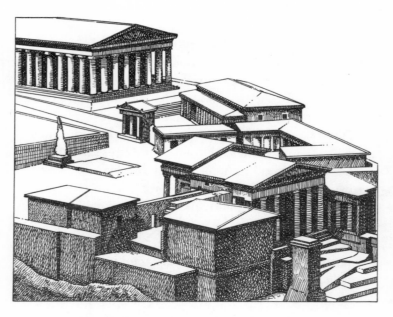

*The roof of the Parthenon was of wood covered with marble tiles; the frieze and other sculptured areas above the columns were painted in red, blue, and gold. This famous temple atop the Acropolis at Athens must have appeared quite different in ancient times from the pale ruins of today. This is a reconstruction.*

discussing politics had developed a philosophical system, which from then on would have been known as "cracker-barrelism."

Porticoes and colonnades played an important role in the education of the ancient Greek, whose schooling grew out of his participation in public political assembly, in religious ceremonies and celebrations. He would have listened to public recitals of Homer, would have learned at the theater and in the many hours of talk and philosophical discussion in the marketplace and colonnade, or, as a younger boy, at *gymnasiums*.

The gymnasium can be said to be the ancestor of the schoolroom, and in some parts of Europe today it is still the word used for a secondary school. The word "gymnasium" comes from the Greek word meaning "to exercise naked." The young boys of Greece exercised and wrestled (another word for a public athletic place was *palaestra* from the Greek "to wrestle") in the nude. Originally the gymnasium was the outdoor exercise yard, the athletic training field. Around the outdoor exercise space a series of small rooms and, usually, porticoes were built for shade and talk. Some of these rooms were probably used as storerooms, but some possibly as classrooms. In at least one rediscovered gymnasium writing has been found on the walls, but whether written for a classroom or as graffiti on a storeroom wall remains a question. Nevertheless, these rooms and the porticoes for discussion seem to be some of the earliest classroom spaces as we know them today.

Greek houses faced inward, presenting a blank wall to the street. Large or small, they all contained some kind of courtyard space. Greece was one of the ancient cultures in which women lived a secluded life; they did not take active part in men's activities. In most city-states they had no legal standing; they were not expected to be present — if they valued their reputations — at dinners or entertainments.

Opinions differ as to how most women were treated at the domestic level, but it can be assumed that courtyard space was important to a wife. It was her outdoors. Not for her were the public places or the markets (in Athens it was customary for a man, accompanied by his slave, to do the household shopping), or sports events or dancing.

Courtyards, then, can be thought of as spaces we have inherited from societies influenced not only by climate but by customs and proscriptions followed thousands of years ago. Do we also inherit traces of old scents and ancient auras? *Are* courtyards feminine and sports arenas masculine? Will they always seem one or the other?

Once we are aware of the Greek's preference for outdoor living, for looking *at* his buildings, and for taking part in public celebrations, we see these ingrained traits, like fine but strong characteristic threads, running through the patterns of Greek style. They were factors that influenced the creation of the Greek theater, a very early model for our own, after it was moved indoors by the Romans. The settings of many temples and their attendant buildings, chief elements in early city planning, were also influenced. Raised sites were chosen not only out of early habits of building citadels and fortresses on heights, but for aesthetic reasons and with background well in mind.

Less obvious but most important is the fact that because the public buildings were more looked at, with activity going on around them, than used inside, various cities, their artisans, architects, stonemasons, and sculptors, vied with each other to create finer proportions, to become expert in the best and most effective use of material (usually limestone or marble), constantly to improve traditional techniques and to surpass one another in the workmanship of the sculpture, painting, and decoration. It is possible to assume that this small-world competition (for it was a comparatively small world then) did much to establish that perfectionist artistic tradition of intricate variation *within* an arrived-at and accepted ideal form. Again, an attitude quite different from our ideas about change, variations, and progress in the modern world.

It is also likely that this love of outdoor living was a chief factor in influencing the scale of buildings. We say that Greek architecture, before Alexander the Great, had human scale. By "scale" we mean how one comprehends a structure, as well as how the size of the structure corresponds to one's own physical size. Egyptian architecture was on a massive scale. A person standing next to the Pyramids appears in scale somewhat like a person in a photograph standing next to the largest, most ancient redwood tree. The human figure is lost, dwarfed; it is impossible to see the whole person and the whole tree at the same time. In ancient Greece buildings and humans were almost always in comfortable visual and spatial relationship to each other.

In addition, we know that the early Greek city-states were small contained units, with a kind of political balance favoring individuals and concern for human development on all levels, and we know that this was an attitude previously not known in large kingdoms. So a preference for living outdoors, and a philosophy oriented toward the individual (*people*) were the two important influences in the development of a hitherto unknown human scale for large public buildings.

Certainly, when the city-states gave way to princely tyrant families, a change took place in Greek architecture; in time, with the conquests of Alexander, public buildings adapted themselves to a larger-scale world, became more lavish, more monumental, less community oriented, and broke into separate elements that were copied first by the Romans and later by most of the rest of the Western world. But the Greek unity, the architectural relationship to human beings and to nature, was lost.

Human scale has always been spoken of as one of the chief attributes of early Greek architecture. Now, in an age when we seem to be losing more and more a sense of human scale, this Greek characteristic evokes much nostalgia and admiration from many who dislike alien immensities next to which, or in which, one feels lost or dwarfed. It may be important to remember when thinking about scale and about civilizations, ancient and modern, that human scale changes in relationship to basic attitudes about humanity. Throughout history changes in aesthetic ideas of scale have usually *followed* changed ideas about ourselves and our place in the world. So it would seem that in matters of scale all society is involved, not just the current architect or group of builders.

The Greek facade, with its porticoes and colonnades, is common in the United States today. Banks and campus buildings, built in the 1800s, are the most usual examples. Some are well-executed, some poorly executed, but, take away the conversing Greek, his religious and moral philosophy, the hot sun or the sudden shower, and take away in the background the sacred, unentered inner sanctuary, where the spirit of the god lived, and *all* copies are facades and no more.

Yet we owe more than facades to this civilization in history. Among those things we *see* all the time are the layouts of many of our college campuses, our playing grounds, our theaters, our town and city planning wherever and whenever it has been possible to make it enjoyable, harmonious, and balanced geometrically rather than rigidly symmetrical. Among those things we *feel*, we owe the Greeks our recognition and love for the beauty found in unity, simplicity, and proportion.

Looking back in time, we see that the Greeks were not so much builders in the sense that the Romans, who came later, were, as they were intellectual designers, creative

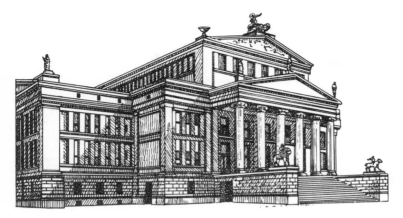

*Revival*

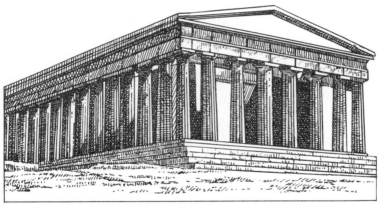

*Old*

*Attempts in modern centuries to re-create the proportions, the classic simplicity, and unity of ancient Greek architecture have resulted in little more than facades and details, as this comparison shows.*

mathematicians, craftsmen, and artists, who thought through and arrived at principles of universal truth, who worked *within* ideals. If we were to think in terms of music, we might say that the essence of ancient Greek architecture is not that of single notes strung together or melodious cadences, but of the chord — each element in an essential and balanced relationship, and none extraneous.

# Prototypes

T he Egyptians lived and created in the shadow of the Pharaoh; the Greeks within the aura of protective gods; and the Romans within the powerful framework of the State, which honored the gods so that in turn the gods might honor it.

The difference between the Greeks and the Romans in relationship to their gods may seem a subtle and minor point. It is, however, important to understand, for in architecture it had far-reaching consequences. The Romans built to honor the gods and to identify the State in an impressive way with their rituals, but also to please and shelter human

*Roman aqueduct (Pont du Gard, Nimes)*

beings. Interior space became a place for people and their day-to-day activities, for people to inhabit, to move about in (not outside and around as with the Greeks); a place in which to transact business, to administer law, to hold entertainments, to decorate not only to honor the gods but to record human accomplishments as well.

It was this desire in Roman society that made the arch an important building element for them. Their architecture tells us that they must have realized early that the arch would serve them well.

The Romans were empire builders. In the course of their

history they conquered an area that ranged from Britain and Spain in the west to Egypt and Syria in the east. Obviously, an enterprise of this size is not governed from a street corner or from an arcade, an agora, or even from one of a series of rectangular, low-roofed, partially open-air buildings. Forms and spaces that had proved ideal for past civilizations appealed to the Romans only in part. There had not yet been developed the kinds of spaces that lent themselves to the conducting of Imperial business.

So as the Roman Empire grew, the complexities and importance of large-scale commerce called for open, large-scale interior spaces that could be enlivened by the hustle and bustle of much human traffic and activity. Law courts needed impressive, high-ceilinged chambers; extensive, many-chambered, roofed-over spaces were needed for public buildings and for such popular diversions as the public baths; vast amphitheaters and arenas were needed for entertaining the tax-paying populace. Palatial spaces were required for the Imperial entourage, and public buildings had to be, on the outside, impressive and monumental reminders of the State — its stability, its wealth, and its power. Armies returning home to Rome from the far reaches of the Empire needed monuments to acknowledge their victories, and they must march into a city that was a place of importance, of pride, of grandeur, a "capital," the first real capital city in the sense we now use the word.

This is not to say that a small group of early Romans sat down together one day and said, "Think of it! We are going to be empire builders! Therefore, we will need vast, impressive interior spaces, monumental buildings, and enormous public places. We'll need engineering feats that will supply water for our public baths, and we'll have to plan for other necessities, such as roads for transport, roads that will carry not only our armies, our goods, and our horses and chariots, but will link us to outlying areas. In fact, we must have a capital city that will serve as an example for other cities to copy on a smaller scale elsewhere in the lands we will conquer. Obviously we're not going to get by with columns and beams and massive walls to hold up the roofs. We need to figure out some ingenious variations and ways of building with this arch form we've got here. Perhaps it will give us the kinds of spaces we want."

Nothing like this ever happened, of course. What did happen was that as Roman civilization developed in its own particular way, and as the Empire spread, Imperial needs developed quite naturally and inevitably. Then, bit by bit, solutions were sought and were found. Whether the Romans as a people had, to begin with, an unusual ingenious aptitude for engineering and a sense for structure, or whether their abilities in this area became highly developed because of needs generated by their particular society, we cannot know.

For themselves, in their own time, the Romans were able to carry miles upon miles of roadways and water pipes on arched aqueducts. They created fabulous domelike ceilings which they then adorned with extravagant painting. They produced buildings with multiple, high-ceilinged rooms, niches large enough for statuary, huge amphitheaters with supported rows of seats in tiers (the Greeks needed to choose a site that sloped because each row of seats had to be supported by solid earth), and all these arch-born structural innovations made it possible, not then, but thousands of years later, for architects and other peoples in other cultures to envision the possibility of creating the great Gothic cathedrals.

In opening up interior public space, the Romans were the first of the ancient civilizations to utilize space in the way we use it today and for somewhat the same purposes. Space was used as volume, to surround man, to enclose him, and to make his activities effective, functional, ordered, and comfortable.

The Romans also introduced many of the construction techniques and principles we use today. They invented concrete — a mixture of sand, gravel, pebbles, chippings of stone mixed with a cement of lime and water. Among other advances, their use of the arch form put high ceilings and second, third, and fourth stories on the architects' drawing boards. They built skillfully and for the ages. Many of their public buildings outlasted their civilization and stand today to be seen and studied as an important record of life in the centuries of their Empire.

Since the gods were no longer the *only* direct motivation for existing and doing, another subtle change came about. Society, in the form of the State, took over the job of law, order, and discipline, three basic characteristics of Roman civilization. Morality, which had once belonged entirely to the discretion of the gods, now was shared by society and its rules.

We are more apt to see Roman life and building *realistically* and Greek life and building *idealistically*, for in Roman building much is familiar, and even where details, decoration, size, and form may be ancient, strange, or outmoded, we still have a *sense* of the familiar. Perhaps this is because the Roman mind and society, although by no means similar to ours, can be thought of as a parallel civilization, and as a result the modern mind can come closer to understanding — without necessarily approving or disapproving — Roman attitudes, activities, motivations, aesthetics, rituals, entertainments, business, and justice.

Certainly the Romans built many public buildings which today we see as prototypes.

When the Romans arrived in Asia Minor in the second

century B.C., they (with the exception of some citizens like Cato the Censor, who hated everything Greek) were so taken with the sumptuousness of most Hellenistic art that they began to import almost all of it into Italy, along with the Hellenistic artists to design their temples and public buildings. But since the architecture of the late Hellenistic period was no longer the early, unified, stylistic whole we now think of as pure Greek, the Romans did not continue the essential spirit of Greek buildings and cannot even be considered to have progressively corrupted the originals.

It was, rather, a capture of those design elements that appealed to Roman taste. Liking magnificence and size, they took a dim view of the early, smaller, simpler Greek temples and passed them by.

So we cannot say the Romans copied from the Greeks, even though superficially many elements of Greek architecture can be seen in the ancient Roman buildings, just as many of those Greek and Roman elements can be seen in buildings around us today.

The form of the Roman *basilica*, an important building that served both as a court of justice and a business exchange, was inspired by the porticoed buildings of the Hellenistic East, but the Roman deftness with the arch and the knowledge of vault and timber truss construction turned the interior spaces into one of the most significant prototypes of ancient times, for in its new spatial concept we find the ancestor of the Christian church. Basilica space, which was open — allowing for the movement of a person rather than functioning as a sanctuary for the gods — and the basilica form — a rectangle or oblong capable of holding large numbers in the congregation — obligingly lent itself to the tenets, needs, and philosophy of the new religion when Christianity, in the fourth century, became the legal State religion of the Roman Empire.

*Roman engineers and architects, using the rounded arch form,*
*developed the great vaults shown here. It was variations of these*
*vaults that gave the Romans the capacity to span vast areas,*
*making possible the characteristic large, high-ceilinged spaces.*

But even before the legal advent of Christianity, a significant change had taken place in the building of temples.
Temple space had opened up. No longer was it only a sanctuary. Not only priests but the individual had a place there.
One has only to juxtapose an Egyptian, Greek, or any other
ancient temple plan against the Roman temple and the
Roman basilica to see how the individual had moved into
the internal space. Even when they used elements of Greek
style — columns or colonnades — the Romans did so in ways
and in combinations with other structures that did not bar

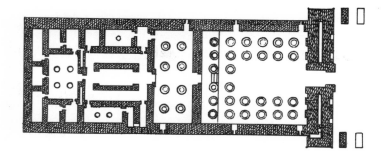

*Egyptian*

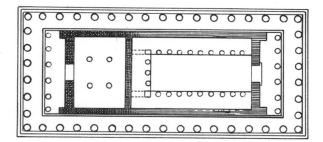

*Greek*

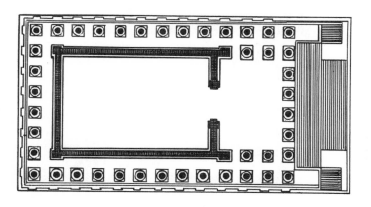

*Roman*

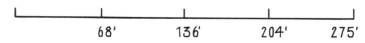

| 68' | 136' | 204' | 275' |

A comparison of Egyptian, Greek, and Roman temple floor plans
clearly shows the changing character of interior spaces. For the
Roman, temple space was also civic space.

the public but encouraged people to move about in the spaces that were created. These spaces were typically Roman — vast, ordered, and symmetrical — all adjectives that could also be applied to the Empire itself.

A recognizable Roman prototype almost unchanged through the ages, but one that has lost its original meaning for us and now exists chiefly as a monument or memorial, is the *triumphal arch*.

For the early Romans, the triumphal arch had a significance directly related to their way of life. Growing empires

*The glory, the conquests, the marching men, the bloodied spears, the clanking chains of the prisoners, even the ancient city has disappeared. All that remains is the triumphal arch, now a model for monuments and memorials.*

have victorious armies, and victorious armies come home from afar, to march in all their panoply, to receive the cheers and welcome of the public, and to give thanks publicly to the gods. So the triumphal arches were essentially gateways, but this meant more than that for both the armies and the public.

Rome was a nation of warriors as well as of builders, and what could be a more thrilling sight than the spectacle of a great army marching *through* a monumental arch, down a broad avenue, long lines of foot soldiers abreast, banners flying, horses prancing, all driving before them captured trophies of war and hundreds of prisoners in clanking chains?

If you were a Roman soldier, the triumphal arch would have a special meaning for you. It served as a sacred gate, for courage in battle and military successes were not considered individual accomplishments alone, but were always acknowledged as due to the grace of the gods. As you passed through the arch, you would probably leave your bloodied spear on its inner wall. In doing so, you were cleansed and released, symbolically, from the destructive forces necessary to wage war, and the leaving of your weapon also signified a return to everyday living.

The *amphitheater* and the *theater* are types of Roman buildings that relate more closely to modern life. Both are used today for the same basic sort of activities, though the nature and manner of Roman performances were flamboyantly different. The Colosseum, an extraordinary engineering feat for its time, is an easily recognizable ancestor of the modern sports stadium. The entertainments that took place there belonged to the ancient world, not to ours. By our standards they were excessively bloody and savage, pitting man against man, beast against beast, or man against beast. This is made more obvious by the Latin word

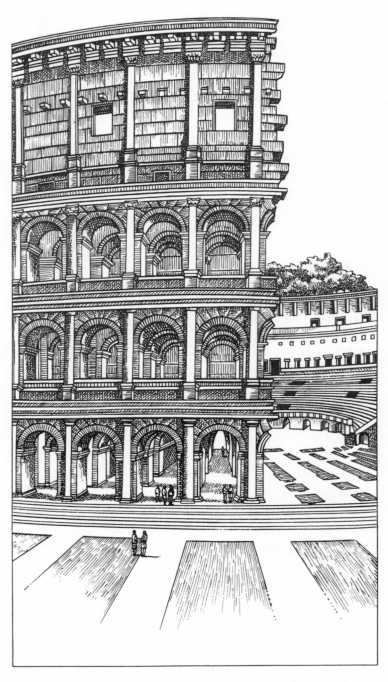

*Though materials used and details of architecture have changed somewhat since the completion in the first century A.D. of the famous Roman Colosseum, the spaces and the arena form so familiar today have changed hardly at all.*

*arena*. It means "sand" or "beach," and is used because the center, the fighting space, was strewn with sand to absorb the blood of the fighters.

Beneath the arena were the vaulted dens for the wild animals. Four great arched stories supported the tiers of seats similar to the banked tiers of seats in our stadiums. The whole was honeycombed with stairways, ramps, and passages, all familiar spaces and forms today. Water pipes (still existing) were used to flood the arena for naval exhibitions held there. Although we flood our arenas for ice-skating, we can get some idea of how large and adaptable the Colosseum was by imagining ships inside instead of ice-hockey players.

The Greeks built stadiums and designed theaters long before the Romans, but their tiers of seats around a playing ground or stage were open-air, of necessity arranged on or built into the slopes of a hill, which provided a natural incline for viewing. Sometimes the top seats were built up with masonry, but that was the extent of the engineering.

The Greek theater, like all ancient Greek artistic effort, was closely tied to religious life. Dramatic performances took place during the numerous, almost constant festivals devoted to the gods, and performances or athletic games usually began with a purification ceremony and offerings to the gods. One has only to compare the Greek theater with the Roman to see again a simple and profoundly religious creation burgeoning in Roman hands into a complex engineered structure, the prototype of our theater today.

In an early Greek theater the spectators sat in a sloping semicircular area — the *theatron* or "seeing place." In front of them were special throne-like stone seats for special personages of the priesthood. Facing the audience was the *orchēstra*, the "dancing place," where the Chorus sang and danced. There was a kind of wooden stage from which a single actor (later two or three) would hold a dialogue with

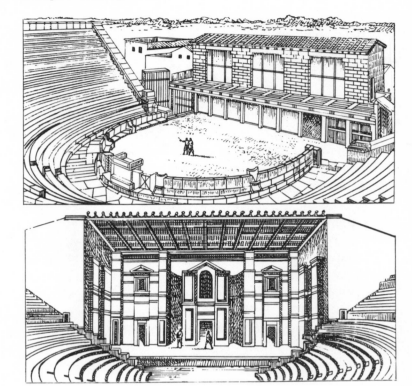

*The Greek theater (above) was an outdoor theater, the seats built into a natural slope; Roman technology enabled the Romans to move it indoors (below), with a stage and tiers of seats resembling those of today.*

the Chorus. There was also added later a wooden *skēnē* used for a dressing hut or storage space, which included a stage of wooden planks, the "speaking place."

The Romans took from the Greeks most of the basic theater elements — the idea of the orchestra, the concave terraced seats, and the area behind the stage — but since the Chorus, which dominated Greek drama, was not a factor in the Roman theater, there developed some few differences in the kinds of spaces needed because of different dramatic usages.

The *skēnē*, the Greek word from which comes our word "scene," referring to a wall that backed the Greek stage, had been plain. The Romans turned it into a rather more elegant background made up of columns and niches for their statuary, but the Roman theater still lacked scenery as we know it. It was the Romans, however, who introduced the theater curtain.

The stage was enlarged, and so was the backstage area, as more elaborate productions were planned by the Romans. Once it became clear that the entire structure need not rely on the shape or incline of the site but could be built from the ground up by erecting structured, supported tiers starting from a level or flat space, the way was opened for buildings of any shape and for more innovative spaces. Restaurants, foyers, and promenades were added — all recognizable features of the art and theater complexes of today.

Even if other historical sources had not informed us, the Baths of Caracalla would certainly have suggested that the Romans were taxpayers like ourselves, apt to be more content and less ill-natured and grudging about supporting the State so long as there were public amenities, such as parks and social-activity buildings, to be seen and enjoyed by the citizens.

A reconstruction from ruins shows the Baths, or *Thermae*, to have been a powerful and complex space conception, one which has bequeathed to us certain kinds of spaces seen and used in many of our best-known public buildings. The Baths were a focus of public life. They were centers for business, exercise, and culture during the day, pleasure and entertainment in the evening. Architecturally, they were the first buildings of multipurpose interior space done on a grand scale. The vaulted halls and the vast complex of rooms and courts were laid out in a park. There was also a running track, a grandstand, and a wrestling arena. Rooms included lecture spaces, small theaters, and early-type libraries, massage rooms, and even dining areas.

These large spaces — the *volume*, the uninterrupted voids spoken of earlier — were made possible by the use of *arch and vault* construction.

The influence on architectural form of social and technological pressures in a given society can be pervasive. Probably the oldest city pressure in the world is crowding, and the resulting shortage of space, which called forth the many-storied apartment houses of today, just as inevitably brought about the Roman prototype two thousand years ago.

In the ancient world, however, the reasons for shortage of space were somewhat different. The Romans were always conscious of defense, and usually a Roman city was surrounded by walls, which defined its form and limited expansion. Space had to be kept clear on both sides of the wall. On the inside, troops needed a wide area in which to move quickly in order to man their posts. The space also was a protection against fire from incendiary missiles, since it was empty of anything important to burn. Outside, a wide space was kept clear for setting up a booby-trapped obstacle course for an attacking army in wartime.

Restricted by defense considerations to an enclosed city, with little opportunity to push outward or around, Roman builders went up. At first they tried two and three stories, eventually five.

The Roman apartment houses were made of brick. They were called *insulae*, and like later apartment houses they sometimes filled areas of a block or more. They also varied in quality of construction, type and stylishness of apartments. Some insulae turned rather quickly into slums of poorly built, dark rooms; others provided large and comfortable quarters. Some were jerry-built, sometimes dangerously so. According to a number of ancient writers, there were many complaints and numerous occupants

The vast, magnificent, varied, and interrelated interior public
spaces, as seen in a reconstruction of the Baths of Caracalla,
were the first of their kind in the ancient world.

killed in a rather large number of scandalous collapses and
fires.

If we were on the streets of Rome, looking for an apartment, we would choose one at street level. At street level
were the most desirable and most expensive apartments,
not — as is the case today in apartment houses with
elevators — on the higher floors. However, the slum and the
tenement house must, unfortunately, be added to the list of
Roman prototypes.

Aspects of Roman character, attitudes, and ideals are
revealed over and over again in Roman houses. Like the
Empire, the houses were organized and well planned.
Symmetrical relationships were profoundly studied also,
and authoritatively passed on. They showed the love of
measurement so characteristic of the Roman outlook. The
relationship of one room to another was well thought out,
and rooms were grouped and connected by doorways to
form apartments or suites, which made it possible to move
through several rooms without crossing and recrossing the
center court. Actual passageways and corridors, as we know
them, did not appear until much later, in the seventeenth
century, and then in England. They were never a part of the
ancient world. Each room had a specific use, with an exact
and correct orientation to sunlight, heat, and cold.

These are some of the admonitions from *The Ten Books on
Architecture* by Vitruvius, a first-century A.D. Roman architect and writer:

> Winter dining rooms should have southwestern expo-
> sure, for the reason they need the evening light and also
> because the setting sun . . . lends a gentler warmth to
> that quarter in the evening.
> Bedrooms and libraries ought to have an eastern ex-
> posure, because their purposes require the morning
> light, and also because books in such libraries will not
> decay. In libraries with southern exposures the books

are ruined by worms and dampness . . . which breed and nourish the worms and destroy the books with mold.

Dining rooms for Spring and Autumn to the east, for . . . the sun as he goes on his career . . . to the west leaves such rooms at proper temperature at the time when it is customary to use them. Summer dining rooms to the north because that quarter is not burning with heat . . . . Similarly with picture galleries, embroiderers' work-rooms, and painters' studios in order that the fixed light may permit colors used in their work to last with qualities unchanged.*

In Rome, as in every era and every society, there was not always aesthetic agreement about building. As a matter of fact, in the early days there wasn't even agreement that aesthetics should be given any consideration at all.

"Cato the Censor, a typical republican of the second century B.C.," Pierre Jacquet in his *History of Architecture* tells us, "maintained that it was necessary in a growing city first to pave the watering places, provide drains, build aqueducts, and make roads before thinking of building tiers of theater seats in the Athenian fashion."

Rigid and pragmatic as were the views of Cato the Censor, they must have been shared by many others, for the engineering solutions to practical problems are the heritage for which the Romans are justly famous and, one might say, revered. The irony is that the ruins, particularly of some of the aqueducts with their rhythmic lines of arches, are now considered — even aesthetically — some of the Roman Empire's finest works.

*Marcus Vitruvius Pollio. *The Ten Books on Architecture*. Trans. M. H. Morgan. New York: Dover Publications, Inc., 1960.

# Naves, Aisles, and Apses

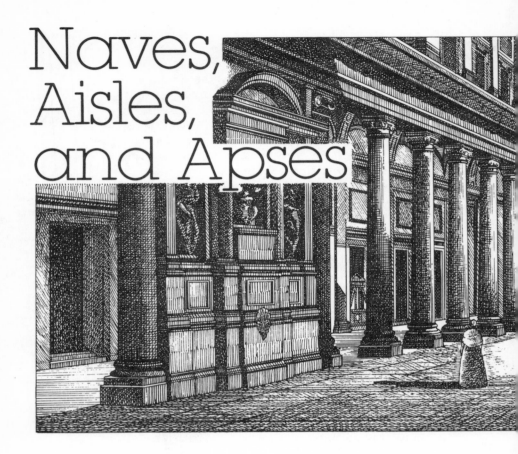

The Romans legalized Christianity in the fourth century. Before that, Christians had secretly gathered in the houses of like-minded friends. In hidden areas, usually in small groups, they celebrated quite naturally in the round, perhaps around a "holy" table, where the word of God was proclaimed. Now, however, they began to feel the need for larger spaces to accommodate increased participation in the ritual. Although worship in the round continued for a time in some early churches, there was at hand one building which was the most practical of the known Roman structures of the time for housing a con-

70

*Basilica Santa Maria Maggiore (Rome)*

gregation. As it turned out, it was also very well suited to the liturgical needs of the Christian service. This was the Roman *basilica*.

The basilica was a public building used for the administration of justice, the transaction of business, and occasional large social events. It was quickly and successfully adapted to Christian needs, and as a result the Roman influence is implicit in all the main structural elements of the Christian churches today — arches, piers, and vaults — and in the general floor plan — the *nave*, that central part of a church planned for the use of the congregation; the *aisles*;

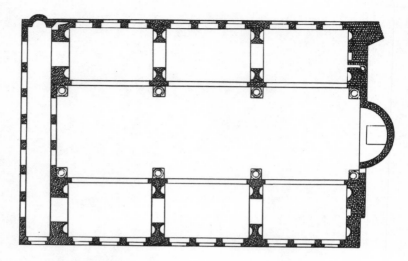

*Because it adapted well to congregational needs, the Roman basilican form served as a model for many early Christian churches.*

and the *apse*, a half-domed, semicircular, recessed space at the end of the nave.

Time, as always, brought variations — but the original basilica building was large, with a wide central aisle and one or more colonnaded side aisles on each side and an apse at one or both ends. In Roman times legal business took place in the semicircular apse. It was then called a Tribunal for Judges and contained a judge's seat centered and flanked on each side by jury seats and an altar used by the Romans for pronouncing auspices or omens. The basilica-to-church adaptation turned the judge's and jury's place into a *chancel* for the priest and the clergy, and the altar was rededicated to Christian use. The Roman populace used the space that is now the nave and the aisles of a church to stand and walk about in. The Christians used that same space to seat the worshipers, who were set back of a low rail.

These adjustments gave the wide aisles and the continuum of spaces a definite direction. For the first time, man's path *inside* a religious building became a primary architectural consideration.

When the Greeks built a temple, their first thought was to make a sacred place for a god, a "house," but, as we have seen, a house that would conceal and sanctify, a space, enclosed, mysterious, undisturbed by the comings and goings and congregating of the public. The Egyptians, too, considered a temple a mysterious place where, if all went well with the care of the god's statue, the god might come to inhabit it. There was need for the activities of the priests and for buildings that were impressive, but no need for space for public congregation. The Christian church, which has also been called a "House of God," was conceived, however, as a *place for people to gather together for communion and prayer.*

When the Christians took over the Roman interior spaces of the basilica to use the basic form for their churches, it was because basilican space already represented social and congregational movement, but the scale, as in most Roman buildings, was overwhelming for an introspective religion based on spiritual love and compassion for humanity. The Christians of those early centuries after Christ tended to reduce the scale of the basilica, but aside from this we find what appears at first to be few differences. These few differences, however, were enormously important.

According to Bruno Levi in *Architecture as Space,* if we compare a Roman basilica, Trajan's (A.D. 53-117), for example, with one of the earliest Christian churches, such as Santa Sabina built in Rome in the fifth century A.D., we find that the Christian architect made two essential changes in the general scheme. He eliminated one of the apses, and he shifted the entrance to the short (front) side of the building. In doing so, he broke the mirror symmetry of the rectangular space, leaving only a long axis, which then became a direct line for the individual's eye, and for his footsteps as well. Visiting the Basilica of Trajan, Bruno Levi points out, you would have entered from the long side; opening up before you would have been a double colonnade so broad that your eyes could not have encompassed it. You would have felt left out, immersed in a space that you were able to walk through and leave, admiring but nonparticipating. In the church of Santa Sabina, on the other hand, you would have been able to grasp the whole of the space. As you walked, you would have been accompanied by a rhythm

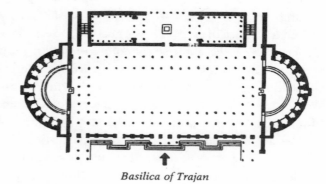

*Basilica of Trajan*

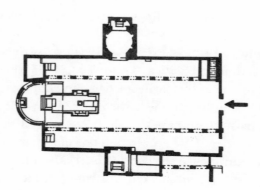

*Church of Santa Sabina*

*Comparison of floor plans.*

of columns and arches. You would have had a feeling that
everything had been designed for the path you were following. You might also have felt yourself a part of a space that
had been created for *you* and had meaning, not incidentally,
but essentially because of your presence. The Christian
bridal procession emphasizes this pathway toward the altar
and the focus of the ritual.

Centuries brought about numerous changes in the Christian liturgy and theological attitudes, and certain physical
changes in the church buildings followed. Yet the basic
basilica plan suffered no radical changes, but grew, like a
person maturing, to take care of new needs. Roman liturgical ideas and theology, followed at first, brought about a
lengthening of basilica space and so introduced the beginnings of the Latin-cross plan — the cross of Christ, with the
uprights longer than the crosspiece — which became common to most churches in Western Europe.

Later the cult of relics imposed the need for many altars
and shrines. Side chapels were increased and consecrated to
saints. The increase of pilgrimages to the places where the
relics were kept brought about the creation of larger spaces
around the choir and nave to allow processions to move
about without disturbing services. Growing national attitudes led to national distinguishing characteristics, de-
pending on materials available, economics, sites, craftsmen
in the area, and local religious and artistic attitudes. Some
of these influences are apparent in the differences in national cathedrals.

There was one other religion, an ancient one, that found
the basilica form to its liking. That was Judaism, the religion whose monotheism influenced most modern religions
and out of which Christianity erupted. That the basilican
theme of social and congregational spaces proved suitable
to the Jews was not surprising, for in the synagogue primary
concern was given to the worshipers who took part in prayer

and ritual. The Jews were the first people in ancient days — though no specific date is known — "to voluntarily assemble to erect a structure for prayer and study, and *not to house a visible God.*"*

The tabernacle and Jewish temple of ancient times were planned essentially as monuments to the glory of God, or as symbolic Houses of God. It was, however, the synagogue, originally created as a meetinghouse for prayer, that developed naturally into a cultural and social center, and also functioned more and more as a common tie for dispersed people. The word "synagogue" is of Greek derivation and means "assembling together."

The synagogue as an element in Jewish life had its beginning in Biblical days, and as architecture it mirrors the complicated, harassed, and uneasy life of the people it comforted. Peace, security, and a sense of permanence and stability often produce a characteristic architecture; it is not surprising, therefore, to find that the active persecution suffered by the Jews throughout their history discouraged them from creating new forms and individualized structures. In fact, through the centuries until the present, though there have been a few buildings of exceptional quality, no characteristic Jewish style of architecture has taken root.

Instead, synagogues have been built in every land, in every known style of those lands, and in all ages; they include the archaic tent of David's time, the basilica of the Greeks and Romans, the vaulted structures of the Gothic, the domed structures of the Byzantine, the numerous revivals and variations in the forms of the Baroque and the Renaissance; even an ancient Chinese temple in Kaifeng, now in ruins, once housed a Jewish congregation.

*Paul Thiry, Richard M. Bennett, Henry L. Kamphoefner. *Churches and Temples*. New York: Reinhold Publishing Corp., 1953.

The Church of Santa Sabina in Rome has retained much of its
original fifth-century early Christian character. A typical
basilican plan shows the nave and aisles and the directed path
leading to a chancel screen (an eleventh-century addition), and
an altar. Behind is the area called the apse. The roof is of timber.

It is interesting to note that Jewish congregations chose the interior space that was the best adapted to their needs, even when the outside of the synagogue often resembled a building built for other purposes; that is, it was the *basilica* forms of the Greeks and Romans, not their *temple* spaces, that were chosen as appropriate to the Jewish ritual and philosophy. It was *people*, therefore, and a religion they were able to carry with them through difficult political and social situations, that influenced, in this case, the ultimate use of a building.

So it came about that as early as the first century A.D., with the pre-Christian Western world still under Greco-Roman dominance, synagogue plan requirements were incorporated into the basilican plan of the period. The apse was a natural position for the Ark; the bimah (reading desk) could be placed directly in front of the Ark or out in the center of the hall; the side aisles provided access to the seating, and the balconies not only permitted an increase in capacity when necessary but also afforded means for the segregation of women, during the ages when this was done not only in Judaism but in a number of other religions as well.

The central-type Greek-cross plan, more common to Eastern Christian churches, was borrowed by later synagogue builders, especially for use by large congregations because more people could be seated close to the central reading desk — which, until the last century, was the center of activity in all services. These two types of plans for synagogues (basilican and Greek cross) have maintained their popularity to the present day.

The building of Christian churches in the West, in the centuries following the so-called fall of the Roman Western Empire in the fifth century, was entirely in the hands of the religious orders of the monasteries, although the actual work was done by stonemasons. The Romanesque style which eventually developed is unusual in the history of architecture because it was by no means a continuum or even a rebirth. It was a new beginning, which took place a long time after Roman structural achievements had been largely destroyed and forgotten. Romanesque is considered the first historical architectural style to represent European civilization after the fall of Rome, and it is this fact that enhances its importance.

Sir Banister Fletcher* likens early Christian building in Europe to the mental image of a giant stumbling to his feet, yawning, stretching, and after a long sleep finding himself surrounded by the untended ruins and treasures of a proud past. He, not symbolically but *in fact*, collects those fragments he needs — stone and rubble — from old pagan temples and great edifices. (Much of the old material was used in the early churches.) He takes sculptured friezes, columns, and capitals, and adds those Roman elements — arches and barrel vaults — whose construction is familiar to him. He reshapes them, cuts them to fit (even the columns), and rearranges them to make the buildings he needs.

What was produced in time, as the readapted elements began to be used and aligned with new discoveries, was usually either a church or monastery building of thick walls made of dressed stone (small-size stones shaped and refined to show a smooth face) held together by beds of mortar. The whole was well articulated (in architecture "well articulated" means about what it means in speech — well joined, coherent, and well expressed). The buildings were heavy but enlivened somewhat by rhythmic sequences of rounded arches, atop each other vertically as well as running in horizontal bands. The structure was generally of Roman-type vaulting and roofed-over rows of columns forming *ar-*

*Sir Banister Fletcher. *A History of Architecture*. Rev. ed. New York: Charles Scribner's Sons, 1963.

*cades*. The character was sober, solemn, and dignified. In this olden Christian era, frivolity, even in buildings, was equated with corruption and sin.

The Romanesque style can be thought of as three hundred years of experimentation with different ways to cover the basilica-to-cruciform church with stone — a roof that would be *fireproof*. It was possible for the Romanesque builder to carry the thick walls of his church to almost any desired height and to pierce the walls with windows (usually narrow and arched-shaped). This gave him sufficient light; there remained, however, the necessity for a covering, a roof. The typical basilican roof was made of wood, and wooden roofs caught fire, from lightning and enemy attacks. Fires caused the structure to fall inward, and many churches were destroyed in this way. The problem for the medieval builder was this: how to use the arch elements in

*This eleventh-century facade shows Byzantine influence and also, banding the apse, characteristically Romanesque rows of round-arched masonry windows.*

combinations that would produce vaults (a vault is essentially a curved ceiling) high enough and strong enough to form a covering of stone, yet still provide light without massive supporting walls to frame the windows.

If the Romans can be said to have played with the theme of the arch, the medieval stonemasons, to achieve their ends, played with the theme of the vault — from Roman barrel or tunnel vault to cross or groined vault to the final pointed-arch, intricate ribbed vault of the Gothic.

When the problem was solved completely and thoroughly after several centuries by a combination of pointed arches, ribbed vaults, and special supports, called *flying buttresses*, the character of church buildings was so changed that a new style of religious building was created. It was one of the most dramatic in the history of architecture and has a familiar name — the cathedral.

# Spires
# in the
# West

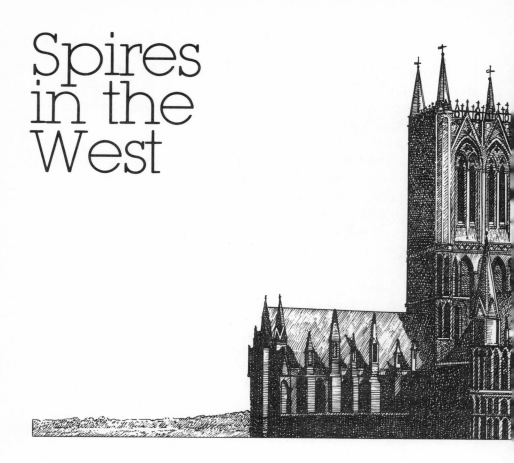

There was mystery in all the ancient religious buildings, and there is mystery in the cathedral — in the mystical heights, the echoing vaulted chambers, in the glowing, whispering colors of the vast stained-glass windows. All are verticals, propelling the eye and mind upward.

To enter a Gothic cathedral is to see space in flight — to feel there is more to this world than the ground we stand on, yet to know the ground is there. It is to have an emotional experience, perhaps a religious response, and, in a strange way, an intellectual experience as well, for one cannot help

82

*Lincoln Cathedral (England)*

but be engaged by the wealth of imaginative technology that characterizes the Gothic.

It is a technology of the greatest significance and drama. Stripping the cathedral, in the mind's eye, to its bare bones, one sees a skeleton of stone, the first skeleton in architecture. (Much, much later, the skeleton of steel, based not on arches but on post and lintel, was to become a familiar building sight in the modern world.) The original technical breakthrough of early mankind, the first building of a wall, which took place thousands of years earlier, was now reversed. Walls, which from that time onward had served as essential supports for any building, lost their significance. Instead, the cathedral builders erected a framework of stone made up of a complex combination of pointed arches on piers for height, and intersecting vaults acting as roof supports, the whole held firm by the thrust of masonry *buttresses* against the sides. Buttresses can be understood this way: imagine propping up a row of books at either end. Ideal bookends would be long-based, heavy, right-angled triangles, the right-angled side holding back the thrust of the books.

The results of this structural revolution (influences of

*Simple buttresses functioning as supports against a thirteenth-century French cathedral.*

*technology*) were far-reaching and diverse. Not only was the entire character of vertical church space changed, but as vaults and buttresses grew more dramatic in form, the exposed structure itself became graceful, lyrical, and ornamental. Vaults grew higher and higher; they were strengthened at the joinings by *ribs* which also proved to be decorative. Almost everything added in the way of decoration seemed to flow naturally out of the basic structure. After piers and vaulting took over as supports, the thick walls of the earlier churches were no longer needed. Walls could now function as lightweight enclosures or fillers which could be decorative or could act as frames for windows of any size. Quite naturally, large stained-glass windows were an answer. Given this new impetus, what had been a minor craft — the making of stained glass — spread and flourished, reaching its height in the thirteenth and fourteenth centuries. During those centuries the well-being and economic status of a considerable segment of that craft's population was improved — a small example of the influence of technology on economic and social factors.

The necessity for dividing up large windows into smaller areas practical for glazing led to a new way of using another architectural element — an upright divider between lights of glass, the *mullion*. "Mullion" was not a new word in a builder's vocabulary, but in the hands of the cathedral builders it was another structural element that developed into decoration, characteristic of Gothic style. Slender and molded, it branched out like limbs of trees to form openwork patterns of stone known as *tracery*. Tracery as decoration became an obsession through the centuries; by the fifteenth and sixteenth centuries patterns were so intricate and ornate that a final phase of French Gothic gives us the word "flamboyant" for the flowing, flame-like designs that ornamented their cathedrals at that time.

The exteriors of the cathedrals reflected the interior structure and were equally dramatic. Buttresses that began as simple projecting supports of masonry in the buildings of the eleventh century developed in the twelfth and thirteenth centuries into bold and striking decorative elements. The "flying buttress" was devised. More poetically named "flying arches," these buttresses are notable and beautiful characteristics of three French cathedrals particularly: Notre Dame de Paris, Amiens, and the cathedral at Beauvais. Decorative spires were added, stone tracery adorned facades and buttresses, to which pinnacles had been added. But these pinnacles, too, had a practical purpose relating to structure. They served as weights to make less massive buttresses more effective.

For the medieval townsman the cathedral as a replica of a heavenly city was a vision in keeping with his surroundings and beliefs. There was a front portal (the gate), the aisles (the streets), the spires and enclosing walls (the turrets and battlements). It was even peopled outside and inside. Many of the facades of the larger cathedrals were covered from top to bottom with hundreds of intricately carved and sculptured figures arranged in rows and niches. Inside, in paintings, wood carvings, stone carvings, tapestries, and the stained-glass windows, was told the Western European story of Christ and the Crucifixion, and the labors, hardships, and spiritual triumphs of the saints and the apostles of Christendom.

Cathedral spaces would not have been possible without the pointed arch; let us try to understand why. The pointed arch was as old as the ancient Persian Empire and was used decoratively, particularly as part of the facades of buildings, throughout the East. It had never before been inextricably tied to other structural elements to achieve the heights attempted by the Gothic builders. The round arch, so loved by the Romans, and by the monks and stonemasons who were the clients and builders of early medieval churches,

presented a problem to the cathedral architect. No matter
what the height or width, the round arch, when used in
combinations to make vaults, was able to cover only a limited and defined area. That area can be seen as the square
*bays* of the early cathedrals. (A church bay is the space
between four piers.) To understand why this is so, one needs
to follow along with an illustration: Rounded arches of
different widths rise to different heights; therefore in order
to make a vault form, the arches had to attain the same
height at their crown. This limited and determined the
ground area covered; it was not possible to cover a
*rectangular* space and also achieve height. Using a pointed
arch, builders could vary the steepness and width of each
element and still make intersecting vaults. This meant that
floor areas of almost any shape could be vaulted, giving
more freedom to the planning. The pointed arch, too, is
much more flexible than the round arch for use in making
vaults, and it creates more graceful forms; its possibilities
can be tested by trying combinations with small models.
Suddenly one begins to be aware of what the medieval
builders discovered when they considered its potential.

Since it was mortals who built, however, the heights of
the cathedral form were ultimately limited by human
abilities. More than a few churches, built too high to be
supported, fell down. The cathedral at Beauvais, in France,
built in A.D. 1225, with a vaulting that reached more than
150 feet, is the most famous of those that collapsed after a
few years. It was rebuilt but never finished. Much Gothic
architecture eventually became so decorative that the organic, structural impact of the earlier cathedrals was lost.
And yet, in pushing his technical knowledge and his aspirations to the full, man produced some buildings of extraordinary significance and beauty, buildings that make a statement about our surprising potential. In a way, cathedrals
touch the heights to which man's aspirations drove and

motivated him in the twelfth, thirteenth, fourteenth, and fifteenth centuries.

A cathedral must be looked at a long time. Both outside and inside there is a sense of history; every cathedral shows indications of different periods, changing attitudes, and developing technology. This is partly because cathedrals, which cost a great deal of money, were usually built, added to, halted, and begun again. Delay was often due to a dearth of building funds. If money wasn't forthcoming from the coffers of the Church's governing body, which sometimes was able to set aside enough to cover several years of building, money had to be raised in a series of campaigns, very similar to modern money-raising campaigns. When times were good, work was rapid, but if bad times diminished interest, sometimes centuries of continuous off-and-on money-raising and building went on before a cathedral could be called finished. This explains the differences in styles in many of the medieval cathedrals, for each addition was built in the style of the time, which did not seem to bother the master masons who created the designs.

This is another indication that one can never underestimate the power of *economic* influences on architecture, but *people* and their attitudes and Christian beliefs were also responsible for the character of the cathedral. Even if the technology of cathedral building had been understood earlier in ancient times, it is unlikely that similar church or temple buildings would have resulted, because what was happening technically in the building of the cathedrals could be said symbolically to parallel what was happening in Europe — a combination of situations and attitudes that had never before occurred.

When Gothic was born about the middle of the twelfth century, it came into a world still controlled by feudal power, a world of princely lands and scattered duchies that had not yet coalesced into the nations of Europe. Just as the

*Pointed arches made possible the mystical heights of such cathedrals as this twelfth-century example at Poitiers, France.*

rounded arch forms were beginning to give way to pointed
arches and ever-heightening vaulted spaces, so was a more
modern world beginning to flower and expand. From our
point of view, the Middle Ages may not seem so free and
modern, but, compared with the monastic Dark Ages, a
whole new spirit was abroad. A middle class was emerging,
caught up in trade and commerce. All was movement and
diversification, but also belief in permanence and unity,
wisdom and an authority apart from everyday existence,
which was limited and beset by all kinds of immediate
problems. There must have been a yearning to believe in
unlimited possibilities; it was a time of growth for a new
faith (Christianity), a new system, a new spirit and function,
and the cathedral can be seen as a synthesis of these new
attitudes. There was a rhythm of movement, of searching, of
reaching out in the world, a dramatic conflict of thrust and
counteraction that one likes to think is reflected in the
rhythm of the cathedrals with their changeable sequences
of complex spaces, differing heights, and soaring verticals.

As windows along the side aisles of the cathedrals became
thinner and larger, the windows of the world enlarged also
for the medieval populace. Commerce grew, the expanding
towns flourished, and the old agrarian economy was increasingly overwhelmed yet supported — "buttressed" — by
a life based on trade and industry. The focus of political and
religious power shifted from feudal manors and the
monastery to the bishop and the king. A place was needed to
show the magnificence of man's faith, his abilities and
craftsmanship, and also, on a more materialistic level, the
magnificence of the clergy and the king. In addition, distinct
ethnic areas were emerging, eventually to become nations,
each with its own local variant of the basic Gothic.

The Gothic style of architecture was not limited to cathedrals, but they remain the most obvious and, with a few

exceptions, the outstanding examples of Gothic character and technology.

France is considered the birthplace of the Gothic style of cathedral. It was there during a period of three centuries that churches and cathedrals proliferated and grew into the most dynamic examples of this new style of architecture. The distinction between a church and a cathedral is not size or magnificence, but only the fact that a cathedral is the seat of a bishop, the place where he officiates. The French bishops of the Middle Ages wielded considerable authority; many had been given civil authority over the town or city surrounding their diocese, and some cities had made their bishops heads of the administration. The Church was total authority for an uneducated populace; the masses of people knew only what the Church taught and what their religion promised in the world to come. The cathedral was more than a place to worship; it was regarded by the people not only as their gift to God but as a place to discuss problems and business affairs, and was often used as a building where public events took place. Thus, it came to play a great part in the political and cultural life of the French.

In the symbols and figures chosen for the sculptured portals, doors, facades of the cathedral, and in its windows and interior sculptures, we see a great stone book revealing not only interpretations of the Scriptures but of the life of the whole town. On the main entrance might be represented the various trades, indicating that they could lead one to the city of God; or perhaps lower parts of windows, donated by corporations of the times, would show the weaver, the baker, the butcher, the turner, the field worker drawn in such fine detail that one can reconstruct the tools used in the trades of that era. The representations of flowers were often local flora and *always* French — flowers the people gathered from the fields and knew and loved. Animals, too, had a

*An elaborately carved facade of a French cathedral.*

place on the facades, along with saints, symbolic portrayals of virtues and vices, philosophy, and scholarship. These animals were not all symbolic; there are proud-looking portraits of the oxen which helped in the building by dragging the heavy local stones to the site. The individuality and creativity of unknown French medieval artists are there, too, in the inventive, often witty portraits of monsters and gargoyles — representing Evil turned to stone by Good. When treating the history of God, artists had to follow the strict interpretations of the Church, but with decorative "evils" they could let their imaginations run riot.

Several influences combined to create an English cathedral somewhat different in physical plan and a great deal different in spirit from the soaring French structures. In England the early cathedrals were built as part of monasteries that continued well into the Middle Ages to play an important part in English life. Spaces were needed for the devotions and attendance at services of a large number of monks; the English, as a result, drew out the length of the nave and lengthened particularly the medieval choir area, thus emphasizing the horizontal. Their vaulting is not so high, nor their windows so vast (England is a chilly country). The English did not take to the flying buttress aesthetically, either, usually covering buttress supports with roofs as well.

The glossary of a small book on English cathedrals written in 1883 and dedicated to the Bishop of Albany gives most terms their technical definitions — that is, "mullion" is described as "the upright post or bar dividing two lights of a window," but for "the spire" the definition given is "Elevation of Thought." This neatly captures the spirit of the English cathedral; its interior heights were never as emotionally powerful as the French, but spires, some of the most beautiful in the world, topped both religious and university buildings.

Spanish Gothic showed Moorish influence and was realistically bloody with its religious images; Germany developed a large open middle space, a "hall" cathedral; Italy kept walls for its superb painters to decorate and never quite accepted the essential Gothic structural unities, possibly because Roman building methods were too deeply ingrained. The national differences and some of the reasons for them would run to the length of a book, but it is possible to say that Gothic, which means "of the Goths," or "of the barbarians," became, in the end, an expression all over the Continent of a new, more sophisticated and scientific Europe. It stood as an example of imaginative technology, for solid links between structure and decoration, for scientific strength, and yet it produced many buildings of breathtaking lightness and grace.

# Domes
# in the East

I n the family-album annals of all the Christian churches that we see today, the original pro- genitor of the large assembly or processional spaces is the basilica of the Romans, but the ancestor of the rounded chapel spaces is what was once called the *martyrium.*

The Emperor Constantine in the Edict of Milan legalized Christianity in A.D. 313, but earlier persecutions of the Christian minority in the Roman Empire had created many martyrs, and this had an impact on the first church build- ings. A cult grew up that derived comfort and courage from the veneration of relics that represented the martyrs and

*The Byzantine domes of Hagia Sophia*

their lives. Altars were built on the tombs of saints and, later, relics (bones, fragments of bones, or, perhaps, possessions) were buried there. These sites became sanctuaries; they were round or polygonal and were used as chapels and for special services. They are important because the spaces remained as part of later churches and can be seen today in some areas of Europe as clover-shaped chapels to which the rectangular room and vestibule were added, beginning about the fourth century. This was the combination that became the familiar Latin-cross plan of the churches built in the western arm of the Roman Empire.

This circular and polygonal space, the *martyrium*, is even

95

more obviously a part of Eastern Christian churches. There it was combined with a more centered plan, forming the equally familiar short-armed Greek cross of that area.

While the building of shrines and churches for congregating was going on in and around Rome at a furious pace following the legalizing of the new Christian religion, the city, as the Empire's administrative and social center, was losing its effectiveness. More and more tasks of overseeing administration were needed to follow on the heels of a far-flung military, and Rome was not functioning well as a capital city for emperors who were rarely there.

There were also those notorious "barbarians at the gates" creating internal problems of security, water and food supply, and morale for a city threatened with siege. The astute and busy Constantine, therefore, moved the capital of the Empire about A.D. 330 to the East, to the city of Byzantium on the Bosphorus. The new capital was renamed Constantinople. There an image was created — and maintained throughout succeeding generations — of a ruling emperor who was a great Christian prince presiding over an organized government as well as over institutions that had been granted by God. Every facet of life in the East reflected this centered and God-favored control. The Church, absolute, authoritative, and hierarchical, and the State, imperial and powerful, were as one. Most trades were hereditary; the tools and techniques were handed down from father to son or to the next in family line. Conditions were rigid and controlled. Rarely was an outsider given an opportunity to learn or compete in any skill.

This was not an atmosphere apt to bring about thoughts of cathedrals, with their experimental heights, their diversification of spaces, their spires pointing upward and breaking into the sky. In the East the heavens were thought to surround one, to be holding one beneath a great cup, a symbol of perfection and divinity. It followed that domes, those earthly replicas of Heaven, would proliferate, their exteriors like so many huge hats dominating the landscape, and their cup-like interiors full of symbolism, vibrant decoration, and emotional meaning for the Christians who came to worship.

The domes of the East were a great structural development as well, another prototype that has come down to us. The Byzantine dome is important because it found an answer to a problem that the Romans, with all their engineering skill, had never quite solved: how to cover a *square* area with a round, domed roof. Though Roman domes such as that of the Pantheon were indeed spectacular, they covered only round spaces; whereas the Byzantine builders developed a method of using small inserts of pieces called *pendentives* to transform a square area into a circular base which matched the circular edge of the dome. This is, of course, a simplified description. There were many problems

*The triangular form between the two arches that rise from the pier column in the foreground of this illustration is one of four pendentives at each corner. This form of inset is the technical advance that enabled the Byzantine builders to cover a square area with a round dome.*

of stress and weight to be calculated and solved, but the East was as obsessed with the dome and its possibilities as the West was with variations of the arch, and builders increasingly perfected their techniques.

The Byzantine churches were entirely logical and suited directly to the needs of an Eastern interpretation of Christianity. All elements were grouped around a central square in which the climax of the service took place. This space was covered by a lofty dome. The whole was then enclosed within a square or rectangular space forming variations of the Greek-cross floor plan.

The space, rather than developing as it did in the West for assembly and processionals, simply burgeoned forth in small explosions of other spaces to form bays, also domed. It was not an easy form to alter or enlarge except by adding new replicas of the old. Sometimes it was simpler to add a new church next door, and this was often done.

The ever-widening breach between the two arms of the old Roman Empire — East and West — began showing itself more and more in the appearance of their divergent Christian buildings. Domes continued to be the outstanding characteristic of the East, while vaults, spires, and towers developed in the West. Why? It was a curious split. Here were two areas, not too far apart, both caught up in the fervor of a new dynamic religion, yet the churches that remain show vast and irreconcilable differences of form — churches of solid strength and centered interiors in the Eastern Empire; churches of skeletal, soaring Gothic in the West — not adequately explained by the six centuries of time-spread between the building of the most famous Byzantine church, Hagia Sophia in Constantinople, and the first Gothic-style cathedral of St. Denis in France.

Neither *climate*, nor *site*, nor *materials available*, nor *technology*, nor any combination of these factors proves on

analysis to have been important in influencing basic character. Rather, the religious and social requirements of *people*
were such strong influences on religious building that other
molding elements played a very minor role.

Technical knowledge, at first glance, would seem to have
been responsible for the domes, at least, because Hagia
Sophia was built in the sixth century, long before the West
had even begun to develop the Gothic vaulting techniques.
Even so, Hagia Sophia took the form of a Greek-cross plan at
a time when Western churches clung to the Latin-cross-
out-of-basilica plan, and although its domes are fantastic
structurally and aesthetically, there is nothing in them to
suggest or inspire at a later age a crop of steeples and vaults
in an area no great distance away.

*Climate*, in the form of a constant awareness of the possibility of earthquakes, probably played a subtle role in curb-
ing a tendency to build for great heights which eventually
obsessed the cathedral architects in the West. *Climate* may
also have affected the size and shape of windows, to the
extent that large windows were probably never even
considered. Hot climates and cold climates share a dislike of
large windows — the cold countries protecting against chill,
the hot countries against heat and intense sunlight.

It was the dome shape and the nature of its structural
demands that took precedence as an influence on the form of
the exterior and on the windows as well. In the East, walls
were the thick Roman walls and never in the eras of church
building gave up their position as chief supports. Windows
circled the edges of domes or filled side arches. A band like a
"drum" was eventually developed, and this made a kind of
double dome, ringed with small arched windows.

Although terrain in the East and terrain in the West are
different, of course, there was not enough difference at the
time for *site* to have been an important influence. A more

*An interior view of the domes of Hagia Sophia, once the most famous of Byzantine Christian churches.*

likely explanation of influence emerges, however, if we combine the *site* factor with *people*, their ways of living in an area that was the European edge of the Orient, and their interpretation of Christianity as it related to the dome.

Constantinople, originally Byzantium (now Istanbul), was a Hellenic city, spiritually more Greek than Latin-Roman. The center of all maritime and caravan routes in those ancient days, it stood at a crossroads of cultures, Oriental and Western, and was subject to influences from both. There were at hand many Greek artisans, still active, as well as engineers who were knowledgeable about Roman structural principles. In addition there were the heritages of the Assyrians, Babylonians, and Persians — all early dome builders. In accordance with the dome's symbolic meaning as an earthly replica of heaven, when Christianity entered the religious thinking there, the inside of a dome was the natural place to picture Christ. There, divided from the world by a ring of light formed by the windows, He looked down from the great heights of the center dome's ceiling to a central altar below. In the East the pictorial Christ was not so much the Son of God, or the Good Shepherd, or the Redeemer of the Cross, but Pantocrater — that is, a sacred part of everything, everywhere, the Almighty, a Ruler of the Universe and a Judge of the Apocalypse.

Higher authorities allowed no variations of traditional scenes; no personal interpretations by the artist were tolerated. The Eastern Empire, which lasted more than a thousand years until 1453, kept to a doctrine and ritual accepted as final and irrevocable. In contrast, years of constant warring in the West between Church and State and between Pope and Emperor brought about many changes of liturgical interpretation and gave stimulus to different ideas and experimentation.

Although there was extreme religiosity in both East and West, the Eastern response to religion remained highly emotional, unquestioning, and strongly authoritative. The processional never became a part of Eastern worship; instead, the focus of the service was always the center area of the church. Also, in the East, Christianity was much affected by Oriental mysticism. It acquired an introverted, meditative, and mysterious flavor, and eventually priests alone took part in Byzantine ritual. Ceremonial events became sacred rites, screened from the congregation.

This centered authority and religious orthodoxy discouraged change, and those religious arguments that did take place, although violently engaged in, remained standard as well as continuous. A chief argument, for example, revolved around the question of images. Were sacred pictures or sculptures idolatrous? Were explicit representations of a physical being allowable in the Church? Were *any* paintings allowable? Sometimes it was "yes," sometimes "no," but each time it was a final, absolute decision.

This, of course, affected the way Eastern churches were decorated, and it accounts in great part for the fact that we see more geometric patterns than pictorial figures, and none of the riot of carved figures so characteristic of the West.

The art of mosaic was to Byzantium and Constantinople what stained glass was later to Western churches and France. In the East, colored glass, tile, or marble mosaic answered the need for decorating the vast blank spaces of interior walls, floors, and domes. Mosaic had always been an art much admired by the Romans, but it reached its height about the sixth century when the Byzantine style of architecture seemed most to demand it, possibly in part because it lent itself to portraiture of religious figures but was equally effective in geometric designs whenever the question of imagery became controversial.

The effects of the Iconoclastic controversy, which raged on and off for a century or more, were widespread and lasting . . . [and] exercised the most profound influence . . . indirectly on architecture, in the years to come . . . . Superficially, certain of the paintings in a Romanesque church may seem to resemble those we find in Byzantine churches . . . but the artists were, in fact, pursuing totally different objectives. The scenes and characters in such a church as Hosios Loukas exist in their own right as participants in the divine Liturgy. Thus the complete disinterest in pictorial space springs not from incompetence or lack of curiosity but is a calculated rejection; there is no need to show the Baptist, for example, carefully and realistically planted on the banks of the Jordan . . . because he is not intended to be on the banks of the Jordan but right here in this very church. The logical extension of this sacramental method of representation produced some curious theories . . . which had a direct effect on architecture. Thus a person was not deemed to be really present if both his eyes were not clearly visible, and ideally the frontal position was preferable to all others as being the most suitable for veneration. But when it was necessary that two personages should confront one another, as in the Annunciation, this rule had to be modified and a half profile with both eyes visible was permitted. However, even this adjustment was not always sufficient firmly to establish the connection, and this led to an increased use of curved surfaces . . . which rendered possible the placing of the Virgin and the Angel at an angle to each other. . . . The only scriptural personage who is invariably portrayed in profile is Judas Iscariot, whose real presence was naturally not required.*

Walking into one of the great Byzantine churches, you would leave behind the almost stark simplicity of the exterior as, inside, the heavy walls would surround you with magically light and luminous mosiac; you would walk on floors of inlaid marble in geometric design. Surrounding you and looking down upon you would be the personages of the Eastern Christian story, all in their proper places. Under the great center dome, you *would* feel at the center of a cosmos, totally Christian, just as the church builders had planned. More interesting to us now as we look back is to recognize that the spaces also reproduced in their form — and in what must have been their psychological impact — the thinking of the time about the nature of the universe: The sun and planets moved about the earth, which was at the center. Surrounding all were the heavens.

*Osbert Lancaster. *Sailing to Byzantium.* Boston: Gambit, Inc., 1969.

The Western churches and their story we see today on the Continent, in England, and in the Americas, while the Eastern (Byzantine) church, its interpretations and its architecture replete with domes, spread throughout the Balkans, Asia Minor, and some parts of Italy. Not many original churches are left in the East. Some still exist in Greece and in Armenia, and in Venice the extraordinary St. Mark's is a kind of extravagant dream version of Byzantine style. The great Hagia Sophia became a mosque in the fifteenth century at the time of the Turkish conquest of Constantinople. Its Christian decorations were plastered over or were covered with whitewash. Though it is still possible to see its vast spaces, one responds as if in a museum, not in the way the early Christians must have reacted.

The Russian church with its onion domes is an offshoot of the Byzantine. The early churches built late in the tenth century imported the shallow Byzantine dome, but here *climate* did play an important design role. The heavy weight of winter snows proved too much of a load for the cup-shaped domes. A few collapsed, and the onion dome, so typical of Russian Orthodox churches, took their place.

Although Constantinople was the first *Christian* capital of the world, by the sixteenth century the last remnants of Roman culture there had vanished, and the Byzantine Christian churches were converted into mosques. The city had become, through conquest, Turkish Istanbul, an Islamic Oriental capital, and the domes, like hundreds of hats on the landscape, were now those of Mohammedan mosques. Not only did the mosques proliferate during the centuries after the conquest, but the number of domes on each building increased, so that one city mosque built in Bursa in the mid-1400s managed twenty domes to itself alone.

The mosque is a perfect example of restricted sacred

*If it had not been for the heavy snows of northern Russia, these spectacular and characteristic onion domes might never have been created.*

space. Its general plan was laid down in the Koran, and nothing was to deviate from these directions. There are a hall of prayers, a courtyard, and a minaret tower for calling the faithful to prayers, not once, but for many periods throughout the day. The design of a mosque can clearly be seen to be a result of Mohammedan religious belief in the oneness of God, in personal and congregational worship; the religion also forbade all symbols of worship that might be considered idolatrous. The only symbol (if it can be called that) that is permitted in a mosque is an indication, usually a niche in one wall, called a *mihrab*, to show the direction of Mecca, which *must* be faced when praying.

The form of the mosque hall is determined by this fact. The hall must be large enough to enable many people to stand in long lines facing Mecca; therefore, in building new mosques, architects developed colonnaded (for support) halls of unusual length parallel to the niched wall.

Since the reading of the Koran and a sermon were also part of the service, a pulpit was included. Ablutions, also a part of Moslem ritual, accounted for the ever-present open courtyard containing a fountain, just outside the great hall. The minaret tower, like a vertical exclamation point, is one of the mosque's most recognizable features. It was a necessity as a place from which to sound the call over the surrounding land, reminding the faithful of each one of the numerous prayer periods *decreed* by Mohammed. Again, a strict ruling determined a form and called forth a suitable design of architecture.

In terms of interior form, the domes of the Moslem mosques can be considered small and larger explosions of space. The dome builders continued to experiment with dome shapes, networks of supporting arches, and other means of support. By the sixteenth and seventeenth centuries the walls of the Turkish mosques — like the walls of the cathedrals — played a secondary part in supporting structure and served more as a kind of pedestal from which there arose the sweep of little and big half domes, all flowing into the swelling curves of a great central dome.

# From Castles

The castle was so much a part of the fabric of living in Europe in the early Middle Ages that it is almost impossible to think about the tenth and eleventh centuries without visions of stone battlements, walls with notched patterns of spaces (*crenellations*) through which the defenders might shoot their arrows, towers with slitted windows, behind which the women sat weaving, and massive double doors for rider and horse to enter a great courtyard where the tournaments of knights took place or the armorers repaired the armor and fighting equipment. Or perhaps the picture is that of remote and mysterious towers and walls surrounded by a moat, and a

*Medieval castle*

. . . . To
Country
Houses

drawbridge pulled tight against invaders.

Those are the castles of legend, and though many of similar description existed, they were not the only castles characteristic of the time, nor did they exist in the vacuum to which our imaginations generally consign them.

Castles came in all sizes and degrees of luxury and were the residences as well as the fortifications of the Dark Ages. Some were comparatively small family-dwelling towers; others were great citadels resembling a walled city. Castles and their surrounding farms dominated the landscape of all Europe during the Middle Ages. There were still great stretches of forest, out of which the fertile farming land had been carved. Each farm had to be large enough to feed a family and provide a surplus for the baron in the castle, but the huts of the serfs who worked the land huddled near the castle. There were few roads, but paths wound past the castle toward the occasional walled town. Only monasteries and a few manor houses of the nobility and gentry shared the rural countryside.

Later, as the feudal hold on society waned, there came into being homesteads of small freeholders, or the *yeomen* of the Middle Ages. Between the eleventh and thirteenth centuries the small towns began to grow, expanding in circular form around the church, which in turn became an increasingly dominant force in the lives of the rich and the poor, the barons and the serfs of those eras.

The original castle, however, was little more than a fortified tower of one room. Its site was of primary importance. It usually stood on a hill near some kind of water supply, or it controlled an entrance to a harbor or river crossing. Wherever it was located, its function was primarily military, and it was stark in appearance and spare in living comforts.

As the castle form developed, the group of buildings and battlements began to vary in size and situation, and in use as living space, though the whole continued to function as a stronghold.

The sole occupation of the seigneurs [feudal lords] was fighting. When the invasions stopped they fought each other. These "private wars" were a curse upon the peasants whose ground and crops were trampled and burned. When not fighting, the seigneurs loved rough and violent entertainment such as hunting and hawking. Another favorite entertainment was the tournaments. This kind of combat was a sport and a test of skill, the object being to unhorse the opponent but not to kill him. Sometimes hundreds of combatants participated, and it was no rare thing that some were killed. Poor but courageous knights were able to earn their livelihood by going from tournament to tournament and competing for prizes.

During the long, monotonous winter days, groups of entertainers went from castle to castle: bear-leaders, conjurers, dancers, and above all, singers of poems. These were the "troubadours" who composed their own song-poems or else retold those already made famous. Their poems recounted great military feats of knights real or imaginary.*

As more peaceful times came about, the typical feudal castle evolved into a country (manor) house. Those changes that took place along the way clearly demonstrate how entwined were the lives of the people with the life, growth, and old age of the castle. Spain and Germany covered their peaks with "castles in the air"; Germany alone produced some ten thousand. The medieval castles of France turned into the great châteaux which still can be visited. The Scandinavian castles often changed into ingeniously balanced wooden structures on a series of hills. However, our choice for an example of the castle-to-country-house transformation is the English castle, because the New World eventually adopted some aspects of its plan.

In England about the tenth century two types of fortified dwellings were developing. One was the strategic fort-type castle. The other, built in the countryside, was not so heavily fortified but was usually walled and was called a "hall."

The fact that London had been sacked by the Vikings in the ninth century proved to be a most important event from the standpoint of architecture. The seafaring Vikings influenced the woodworkers of an England rich in timber, and the English now began to excel at the art of shipbuilding.

*A Brief Guide to French History, published by the Louvre, Paris.

This skill in turn carried over to the building of houses; the result was a large timber-framed hall which resembled a boat built upside down, the keel being the ridge of the roof, the ribs being the uprights and the roof supports. A way of using the natural bend of trees to form a timber arch was developed. (Its shape put the accent on roofs; many were beautifully shaped, and some almost rested on the ground.)

The castle builders adapted this structural technique (without using the overhanging roof) to create a central room free of wooden supports and brought into being the Great Hall, which became the basic, animated, living space of the castle. They added a fortified wall, with towers spaced at strategic corners, and a building called a *keep*, which became the military center of the castle. In the early years these units were all together in one building, but later castles, built by the ruling Normans, separated the buildings and spaced them around courtyards; all was then sur-

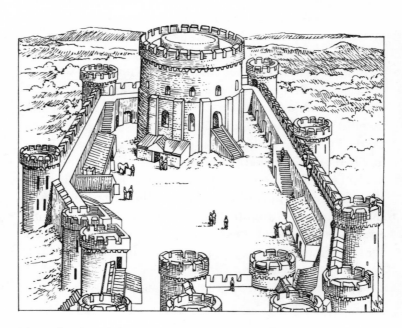

*The medieval castle keep contained the living quarters for the lord and his family, a room for state affairs, and dungeon cells.*

rounded by walls and fortified towers. Castles were provisioned to act as small, self-supporting units throughout a long siege.

Since times were erratic and dangerous, and marauders and enemies came equipped with new and increasingly clever scaling ladders, ropes, springs, thongs, and siege engines for hurling rocks and firebrands, often several walls were built one inside the other. Double drawbridges that could be raised and closed vertically were fashioned, and the castle-with-moat of romantic legend appeared.

There was little that was romantic about living in the interiors, however, or in the surrounding homes outside. Small wattle-and-daub huts roofed in turf sheltered the farm dependents, animals as well as men, women, and children, all under the same roof. The peasants who worked the land surrounding the castle — usually, in today's terms, a large domain (*demesne*) — looked to the castle and its occupants for protection.

In return, the land and everything on it, including the peasants, called serfs, belonged to the feudal lord, knight, or baron. If the lord took his job seriously, he considered the serfs his dependents, his family, though considerably below him in rank. The lord was a sovereign master; he owned the hunting ground, the winery, and what was grown on the land. He administered justice, struck coins, determined what jobs his serfs were to do, and had the power to make free men of his serfs if he so wished. If the serfs took their role seriously, they were loyal and responsive to his every wish. For several centuries the castle remained the visible sign of ruling power; its stones, each one supporting the others, repeated symbolically the social philosophy of the times: each man had his place, like the stones in the walls. If he tried to move from his place, the protective walls — society — would begin to crumble.

Inside the Great Hall smoke from an open hearth in the

center let out through a hole in the roof and blackened the walls. Life was communal. The lord, his family, his dogs, and the higher retainers ate and slept in the same Great Hall, the floor of which was covered with rushes or straw. Lower servants slept in the stables. There was little privacy, comfort, or cleanliness. As a way of maintaining privilege, the lord, the ladies of the household, and their guests removed themselves from the center of activity to a slightly higher platform, a dais at the end of the hall. It was next to this that a kind of kitchen area developed, and, in more elaborate castles, on the opposite side, a few sleeping apartments were hollowed out of the walls for the ladies. This was the germ of the living-dining room, kitchen, and bedroom apartment as we know it. The dais we see today at political dinners, benefits, and social events, where the prominent persons and speakers for an occasion are seated on a raised platform.

Since fire in the center and fires in a few braziers gave limited warmth, eventually, in the twelfth century, it occurred to the more technical-minded to move the hearth from beneath the center hole in the roof to a recess in the wall. From this new hearth the smoke was carried partway up through the thickness of the wall where an opening let it out. With any wind, it blew back in again, but this technical change was the first step in the creation of the fireplace and the chimney, elements that subsequently continued to control the shape and size of northern houses until the advent of central heating and air conditioning.

In a second step in the development of the chimney, smoke was carried out to above the roof in a single large stack and, still later, in a cluster of handsomely decorated brick stacks. Inside, at the hearth, it was discovered that a hood projecting above would catch some of the smoke, and this addition much later, after going through many metamorphoses, became fully decorative rather than fully practical, and turned into the mantelpiece.

Every time the castle was besieged, it was necessary that the cottages outside be burned to the ground so that the marauders could not establish themselves there for a long siege or use the materials to create a huge fire. The families living in them, their animals, and what possessions they could carry were moved to behind the castle walls, which they would help defend. It took, therefore, a long period of relative peace before anyone even considered improving the condition of the huts or thought about ways of contributing to their permanence.

As more peaceful times approached, the castle enlarged its character. It remained behind walls but added a few chambers for some kind of privacy for the lords and ladies. The Great Hall was still the center of life, but now inside the walls it was often part of a separate building that contained only living quarters for the family and their retainers. A chapel, stables, and other service buildings might also be separate from the fortified towers. The knights had returned from what Bernard Rudofsky in his book *The Prodigious Builders* calls their "unholy holy wars" of the Crusades. In their stay in the Orient the Crusaders had become used to color and aware of patterns and artistry. They began to decorate their establishments with rich hanging tapestries for warmth and color and to widen and embellish their windows. Instead of slits, lancet-shaped windows appeared, and wooden stairways came into being. A small space off the gallery of the Great Hall, to which the early barons had retired in order to be away from but still watch the activity, now became a private study with only a peephole to enable the master of the house to check the main hall from time to time.

Altogether, living became cheerier, more relaxed, and

*Prior to the fireplace, the center fire was the focal point in the Great Hall of the castle, but the gentry dined on a raised dais, similar to the one on which we seat distinguished guests today. The timber roofs were shipbuilders' art.*

slightly more comfortable, but it was not until the fifteenth century that real planning for privacy and comfort began, and by then the cannon and gunpowder had made the fortified castle obsolete. Social changes were also bringing about the end of feudalism.

All land was now controlled by the king, and the castle, becoming more and more open with only minor fortifications, was turning into a large country manor, but the floor plan still had one disadvantage. One had to walk through one or more rooms to get to another, or, like the Greeks and Romans, move from one group of rooms to another group by going through a central space. It was not until the beginning of the seventeenth century that corridors and passageways were planned and incorporated. The introduction is credited to Inigo Jones, an English architect who lived from 1573 to 1652.

By the sixteenth century the bay window had also appeared, and wings had grown on either side of the great center hall; the kitchen area developed into a large service wing, and the early retiring place of the lord, and the ladies' private areas became a wing of private apartments.

The Great Hall became a stable element of English homes, but by Tudor times it tended to be reserved for special dining and ceremonial occasions. Family life took place in an increasing number of rooms — winter parlors, morning rooms, long galleries, sitting rooms, studies, libraries, servants' quarters, butteries, kitchens — all the essential architectural spaces of the English country house of the gentry as we know it today.

Eventually even the houses of the poor, which usually lag even further behind all other building, were affected by changes and advances in domestic architecture. By the sixteenth and seventeenth centuries the poor had moved from the medieval hovels of one room to cottages built of timber framing, the spaces between the timbers filled with mud plaster. There were small windows and shutters. Inside, one or two rooms usually had built-in box beds, a few benches, a table, and perhaps a cabinet. A partition often separated the front and back, so that the rear might be used as a stable and barn, for when the peasant moved into better quarters, his animals moved in, too.

Two other kinds of living arose in early medieval times: the monastery complex, and town houses, which began to be built in increasing numbers from the eleventh century on.

The intellectuals of the Middle Ages were not the barons in their castles. The barons were well-educated only in the arts of fighting and in the hunting sports. Those with scholarly inclinations in well-to-do or noble families were absorbed by the monasteries. Monastic orders were, in effect, communities of scholars, book copyists, artists, and skilled craftsmen. A monastic order was self-sufficient, with bakery, brewery, shops, farms, and so on, and lodged many dependents and laborers, from bailiffs to swineherds, who helped protect the complex from marauders. The richer monasteries came to be known as refuges, relatively safe and peaceful islands in the vast, hostile outer spaces of the early Middle Ages. Even in early days one of the occupations of the monks was the copying and illuminating of passages of Scripture and other rare manuscripts. In order to educate potential candidates for monkhood, the monasteries established schools. Eventually, since there was no education except that connected in some way with the Church, other lay people were admitted to the monastery studies, and thus began many of the famous universities of Europe and England.

Those houses that were needed in a monastery complex — the abbot's house, a guest house, and living quarters for the monks — were variations of church architecture, with arcaded courts, or *cloisters*, around which the

*With their arches, arcades, and enclosed central courts, and the aura of quiet and meditation, cloisters still give a visitor a feeling of safety and seclusion.*

rooms were grouped. A monastery kitchen was usually a vast space with a great ring of circular fireplaces. It is the element that has changed the most in transition to modern times. But the dining hall with its long, narrow tables, called the *refectory*, is a recognizable feature of the older universities and colleges of Europe and America today, as are those dormitories which still repeat small cell-like rooms, as well as cloistered courts and many of the libraries.

In contrast to the expensive, orderly spaces of the monastery, the town house of medieval times was several stories high and packed in so close to its neighbors on both sides that it seemed almost to be held upright by them. The upper stories often projected over streets to give more space to the interior. In the North the roofs were steep; in southern climates balconies hung over the narrow streets, almost touching above them. At ground level there was usually a shop and a storeroom. The merchant's family lived above;

children and apprentices and servants occupied tiny rooms under the roof. Stairs were narrow and steep, and the whole was what we would think of today as a nightmare of a fire hazard, since roofs, when not tiled, were thatched, and many houses were built of timber with only plaster and brick used as filling.

The city houses in America today retain the high, narrow, packed-in appearance in the form of the brownstone, though the overhang has disappeared. Gone, too, is the unusually alarming vulnerability to fire. The floor plans of the more elaborate English country houses were eventually copied in the New World, but on a much smaller scale.

The early American colonists left behind in Europe not only the architectural trappings of great wealth but also the carpenters and craftsmen of Gothic times who might have built houses for them. So, for the first arrivals from England, the mud-and-wattle hut came into the picture again, but more briefly this time. Soon, hearing tales of the new land — most of them exaggerated — many more immigrants came, and among them arrived carpenters and craftsmen from France, Holland, and England. They eventually reproduced versions of architecture familiar to them — what was remembered by the colonists from the old country — tempered, of course, by the more severe *climate*, where it existed, by the *materials available*, and by the need for quick completion and use. All this gave the early homes a simplicity and forthrightness associated with New World people in their struggle for survival. A Colonial tradition emerged, a new fashion, which was based on the architecture of a generation *before* in the mother country. News and information traveled slowly in those days, so the architecture was of the sort the colonists had grown up with and had left behind.

Some at least of these houses of the middle seventeenth century in Salem or Boston must have once seemed almost like those of the village streets of

*The harsh New England climate determined to a great extent the architecture of the clapboard house.*

England, with the same many gables, the same steep roof slope, and the same casement sash . . . .

But this half-timber construction, however suited to the English climate, was ill-fitted for the severe winters and the icy northwest gales of an American winter. The wood shrank, the filling cracked, the winds felt out and penetrated every crevice; and, no matter how great the fire which roared in the enormous fireplace, drafts and the dampness of driving rain must have made these houses uncomfortable indeed. Thus, to answer the first great pressing problem of climate, the colonists were forced to their first great modification — the covering over of these half-timber houses with boards, those overlapping boards we call *clapboards* — and at once the entire aspect of the towns changed . . . .*

The French who settled along the St. Lawrence built houses that show, in their hipped roofs and round corner towers, traces of the châteaux and manor houses of France. Their villages must have looked very much like the streets of the country villages back home in France.

In New England, where there was an abundance of wood, houses built of wood were the most common early-seventeenth-century homes in the colonies. These were followed by homes made of bricks. Bricks either came over as ballast in ships or were made in the colonies, one of the earliest industries of the new country. The Dutch of New York and the English of Virginia were especially partial to buildings made of bricks. There were a number of stone houses, also, in areas where stone was plentiful.

The log cabin, which we usually think of as the indigenous house of North America, was actually a work of carpentry not well-known to the English or to most of the early European colonizers. It was introduced to this country by the first Scandinavian immigrants who, with great forests of their own land, had discovered how trees felled on the spot could make a strong, tidy, simple dwelling.

In most of the New England wood houses the floor plan recalled in miniature the English hall, since it revolved around the hearth. There was a main living room, with a kitchen (usually a lean-to) on one side or at the back. As the house expanded, on the other side or above were sleeping quarters. In all cases, the fireplace and chimney determined the center point, or *axis*, of the house. The downstairs rooms

*Talbot Hamlin. *Architecture Through the Ages*. Rev. ed. New York: G. P. Putnam's Sons, 1953.

were placed around this central point, and the upstairs often was used — in the beginning — only for storage. In the Virginia colonies it was common for two great chimneys to rise at either end of the house, allowing for a through-center hall, with rooms placed around the chimneys on both sides.

In the Southwest and California, houses inherited the balconies, the long or casement windows, the shutters, and the courtyards — usually reduced to patio size — of Spain and France. The *adobe house*, however, was *born* in Southwest country. It is suited to a hot, dry climate, since it keeps warm in a mild winter and stays cool in summer. Made of sun-dried brick or clay, and whitewashed, it has a simple U-form with a low-pitched roof of tiles. The rooms surround a patio court on three sides. An open, lower-roofed passageway running around the U gives covered access to the rooms.

Though fortifications against battering rams or cannon

*This facade of one of the earliest types of dwellings of the West and Southwest United States — the adobe house — presents the typical almost-blank front to a hot, dusty road.*

did not call for walled towns or towers, there was a need for the early settlers to protect themselves against hostile attack. In the Dutch colonies, the largest and strongest house built, usually of brick or stone, often was used as a refuge to which all would come in case of trouble. The Spanish built missions in Florida, California, Louisiana, Texas, New Mexico, and Arizona. They were probably the earliest resident fortifications in North America.

A mission, a form of monastery, consisted of a building for a commandant and soldiers, called a *presidio*. It contained offices, a dormitory, rooms, and the armory. In a large courtyard there were also a church with cloister for the monks living there, a dining refectory, a hospital, schoolrooms, storerooms, guest quarters, and workshops for blacksmiths, carpenters, tailors, and other craftsmen. Adjoining were stables and farm buildings, and outside were the stockade and the vast ranges for cattle and sheep owned by the mission. The whole was, in effect, a small rural fort, which fulfilled many of the functions of the Old World castle and monasteries. A third part of the mission complex was the pueblo, or living quarters for Indians who had been converted to Christianity, who, like serfs, did all the manual labor and took care of the large cattle and sheep herds in return for board and religious instruction.

North America never built any palaces or castles, however, except a few imported from Europe purchased by certain millionaires of the 1800s as art or for their antique value and rebuilt stone by stone on American soil. There was no fundamental need in the new land when it was colonized for such structures, for North America never experienced anything closer to an authentic feudal hierarchy than the feudalistic style of the aristocratic landowners of the South, or some of the fortified mission complexes of the West. Nor was there any impulse toward reproducing the vast, extravagantly spacious interiors of some of the Old World's

*A mission complex, one of a series of Spanish outposts, a day's march from one another, established in the mid-1700s in Alta California, now the State of California. These colonial combinations of forts and religious centers were built in the New World to carry the Church and the culture of the Spanish Empire to outlying regions.*

châteaux and palaces. The people who emigrated were not of the great, powerful families; they were of much more modest means with different ideas and horizons. They were ready for a new kind of society, and their houses showed it.

# New View ... and a Return Address

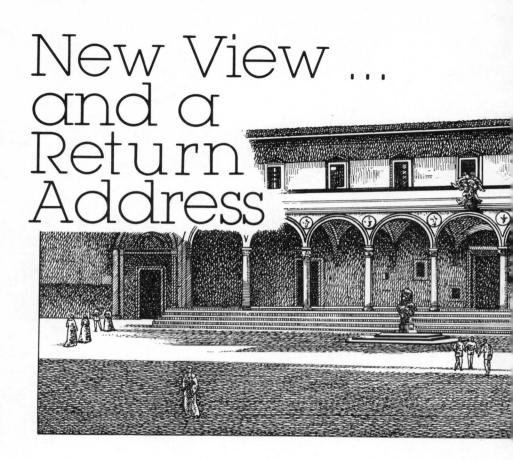

That open-ended period of historic time known as the Renaissance should really be in the plural, because the renaissances experienced by many European countries had their origins at different times, accented different aspects of creativity in the arts and varied in their durations. Yet they shared, from the beginning of the fifteenth century, one profundity and several awakenings, all of which greatly affected the architecture and buildings of the following centuries.

The profundity was a new view of the world and of its place in the universe. For the people of the twelfth, thirteenth, fourteenth, and part of the fifteenth centuries, it was

126

*Foundling Hospital (Florence, Italy)*

a well-established belief supported by the Church that the earth was the center of the universe. According to this belief, the sun, the moon, and the planets, of which five were known in medieval times — Saturn, Jupiter, Mars, Venus, and Mercury — moved around the earth. Outside these spheres was a mystical area of space called the *empyrean*, the highest heaven. This was what the interior of the dome had come to symbolize.

By the sixteenth century, with the publishing of the theories of Copernicus, it was a recognized scientific fact that the earth moved around the sun, that it was only one of the many planets in a solar system, and that the sun, not the

127

earth, was the center of the universe. This was a profound and fundamental change of viewpoint, or viewing point. It was a scientific fact eventually absorbed and accepted by all, but, at the time of its discovery, its effect was not immediate and obvious, and it sowed discord because it originated from "science," and not from a still authoritative Church.

There was much developing scientific and humanistic knowledge about this time. Undoubtedly the new view of the solar system added its considerable weight to the basic forces splitting and cracking the medieval world at its center, for, in time, man's view of himself and of his social and religious relationships changed radically. The course of history suggests that a fundamental change of viewpoint will eventually change the emphasis in the social and political world, and change of emphasis is generally followed by change in the power structure. In this case, since it was scientific knowledge that produced a reality the Church could not counter, power shifted gradually from the central position of the Church to royal and titled personages and individual Popes — in other words, to powerful *men* rather than to traditional institutions. The shocks of these changes and other new knowledge continued throughout the next three centuries, and the world re-formed into a relatively and recognizably modern, though not yet contemporary, society.

No precise date, no sharp line separates epochs. Beginnings and endings flow together: the Dark Ages awake and become the Middle Ages; the Middle Ages continue to expand in commerce, invention, and discovery, and flower into a period of Renaissance. Was the Renaissance, then, still of the Middle Ages? Or had a new epoch begun? Insofar as the general landscape was concerned, the world of the castle was gone. Politically, philosophically, and practically, castles were obsolete. Gunpowder, introduced into Europe in the fourteenth century, and the cannonball — made of stone in the early days — had delivered the final battering to the fortifications (*technology*). Brief but violent and bloody peasant rebellions throughout Europe had eventually put an end to feudalism. When loyalties shifted to a royal banner, away from the now warring, dissident, often wandering bands of barons and knights and away from the monasteries of the medieval Church as a refuge, and as people turned increasingly to fortified towns for protection — (*People* — Political   and   Social) — the   castle walls did, indeed, come tumbling down.

Transition was not graceful, nor was it rapid. In spite of the invention of movable type and the appearance of the first printed books, in spite of the emergent free and independent cities, the rise of the merchant, and the century of the flowering of the great and powerful families, much thought at the end of the fifteenth century was still medieval. After all, in 1492 not everyone was ready to risk with Columbus the belief that the world was round, though there was solid scientific evidence for it at the time. Though the dictatorial powers and pronouncements of the Church were waning, its style, its panoply of wealth and erudition, was impressive, and scientific thought, or, more precisely, alchemist-philosopher ideas, were viewed with distrust. To accept and assimilate new ideas took a long time, and action that was not traditionally and religiously acceptable was taken at great personal risk.

Finally, there is perhaps the most important factor which all the renaissances shared and which greatly affected architecture: the recognition that a person was an individual with potential and creative ability and a certain power of his own.

It is not surprising that the early Renaissance had its birth

in Italy, where there were many independent cities and
where the architect as an individual talent came into his
own.

The general definition of the architect as an inventor — a
person who creates plans, designs a building, and oversees
the means by which it is accomplished — has remained unchanged throughout the centuries. But in the early Middle
Ages, because the master mason — actually the architect —
was considered a layman lacking in knowledge of theology,
he was given none of the distinction, the personal fame, or
the professional prestige bestowed upon the ancient architects by their imperial patrons. For a period in the early
Middle Ages even the word "inventor" had degenerated so
much in meaning that it was used to refer to someone who
denounced a person, gave information. An "inventor" was
an "informer."

In the twelfth and thirteenth centuries the men who
functioned as architects were called cementers, stonecut-
ters, or master masons. By the middle of the fourteenth
century, we are told, the architect's status was higher: he
might own his own house and some of the quarries from
which he would then purchase the stone for a building. He
was also eligible and able to afford at this point to be buried
beneath a tombstone with his name carved on it.

Knowledge of the intricate and complex Gothic structural
system presupposes men of considerable skill, training, and
talent to have been involved in the building of cathedrals,
although almost all of them are anonymous. Usually they
were men from the ranks of the masons who showed creative ability, who had somehow acquired the necessary
technical education, and who were capable of assuming
responsibility for carrying through a complex project. Their
drawings, often on plaster, some of which are still in existence, show excellent ability, and they also made accurate
scale models. Their professional life, however, was quite

different from that of architects of later times. They worked on only one project at a time and were expected to devote themselves to every aspect, including taking part in the actual construction. They had no offices, but traveled to other locations or other countries, when and wherever their services were called for.

If these architects of the Middle Ages were mostly unknown, the opposite can be said of those of the Renaissance. The history of Renaissance architecture is basically the history of individual artist-architects. It describes their individual talents and chronicles their relationships with other architects and with their clients, both of whom were continuously moving closer to the professional and business relationships in operation today.

As the Renaissance era progressed, the idea of individualism seems to have spread into all areas associated with the arts. Even the client-architect relationship was on a more individual basis than it had been in the Middle Ages. In Italy the patrons of architecture included members of the great families — men of cultivated taste, wealth, and power, as well as ruthlessness and determination — Popes who wished to leave a lasting reminder of their reigns, and the city fathers and the Guilds of the free cities. With their church doors and domes, their palaces, their sculpture, their formal gardens, their fountains, cascades, and pools — all considered part of the architecture — they carried on an artistic rivalry reminiscent of that of the Greek city-states, though on a more grandiose and worldly scale.

The results of this surge of individual expression were buildings which, however similar in general scheme, were different in effect and showed the distinct and recognizable touch of the designer.

While Gothic style was still popular in most of Europe, in Italy, particularly in the free city of Florence, the artist-architects were beginning to return for inspiration to the classic tradition of Greece and Rome. However, it was a technological event — the invention of type and the printing press — that influenced and advanced the architectural style that came to be known as "Classical Renaissance." Classic thought had been kept alive in the monasteries of the Middle Ages, and as books and the habit of reading spread, cultivated men — clients as well as artists — were steeped in the classic heritage and tradition. At the same time, Christian religious needs and beliefs and the ideals of a developing humanistic society were at variance with the ancient culture of the old Roman Empire and the religious beliefs of the ancient Greeks. Therefore, Renaissance buildings became, not copies of the classic, but new and original responses that grew out of classic forms. The great Renaissance architects used the vocabulary of the classic tradition, but their creations and their spaces told a story of many new insights, new ways of living, and new ideas about mankind.

For example, by the fifteenth and sixteenth centuries, the time of Leonardo da Vinci and Michelangelo, the idea of the individual had become so important and fundamental in Renaissance thought that even the proportions of the human body were related to architectural theory. Michelangelo himself wrote, " . . . the architectural members derive from human members." This was a far cry from the Egyptian temple, built to cater to the needs of a god, from the Greek temple as sanctuary for a god, or from Roman buildings as symbols of an empire.

The early Renaissance architects broke away from the Gothic search for heights and emphasized the horizontal. A good early example is the Foundling Hospital designed by the Florentine architect Brunelleschi in the fifteenth century. It is usually referred to as the first of the Renaissance style. The Foundling Hospital also demonstrates that to the Renaissance architects proportion, grace, and refinement were of greater interest and importance than the skeletal

*The balustrade, the series of little pillars or columns supporting a handrail, developed during the Renaissance. A distinguishing characteristic of buildings of this period, balustrades are as recognizable as a trademark, even today signaling Renaissance influence.*

power so characteristic of Gothic style. There was also in the Renaissance a profound desire to measure, to define, to establish laws even for surfaces. In a Renaissance building, arches, windows, and doors are repeated in a purposeful pattern and in a mathematical relationship to one another. We see this horizontal rhythm in the fifteenth-century Palazzo Pitti in Florence; in the sixteenth-century house of Raphael in Rome; in the Library of St. Mark's, sixteenth century, in Venice; in the seventeenth-century Queen's House by Inigo Jones in Greenwich, England; in the Banqueting Hall, Whitehall; and in the East Front of the Louvre, seventeenth century, in Paris.

In the Palazzo Pitti we see also the horizontal emphasized by the railings made up of small column-like posts called *balustrades*, which are an invention of the Renaissance and a heritage to us. Balustrades can be seen used as decoration on an occasional Fifth Avenue building in New York City.

They were adapted as a guard railing system for stairways
in houses built in the late nineteenth century, topped by a
*banister* rail, down which mischievous children in Victorian
stories always slid, to the consternation of their proper
parents. The *cornice*, a projecting, decorative molding, finishing off the architectural part to which it is attached, like
an architectural top hem, was not invented during the Renaissance, but was used so much in later buildings in so
many decorative forms that it has become an easily recognizable characteristic of a Renaissance structure. It, too,
emphasized the horizontal.

In Renaissance buildings, behind the rhythmic and
evenly spaced facades, are rooms of various sizes, some
large, some quite small. There are corridors and staircases,
all in mathematical relationship to one another. This is
again completely in contrast to the Gothic interiors, which
are usually frank structural results of the exterior plan or
form.

Architectural historians tell us that Renaissance space is
space that is rational, geometric, that it can be comprehended as a whole, intellectually. These statements are
easier to absorb the more any Renaissance building is compared with a Gothic one, particularly a Gothic cathedral.

It is almost impossible to look at a Gothic cathedral and
not be taken over emotionally by the spires, the towers, the
vast vaults, the sense of a structure built out of a fervent and
passionate belief in a world beyond everyday existence.
Walking through the cathedral, one is alternately quieted
and excited by mysterious heights and the many intricate
and separate effects.

The impact of Renaissance spaces is quite different.
Within a frame exists an ordered world. The effect is of a
whole, which can be understood and looked at in the same
way one comprehends a painting or a sculpture. Bates

Lowry says of Brunelleschi's Foundling Hospital:

> ... the arches, columns, and windows of the Hospital facade [are] set within the precisely defined frame of the steps, side pilasters, and cornice.
>
> Although the method of producing the illusion of [perspective] was different in [a painting] and the building by Brunelleschi [both] were created according to the same principles because their intended effect was the same — the presentation of a visual image whose total form was dictated by a concern for how it would appear to the eye of the human observer.*

Again, the individual is the most important consideration for the Renaissance architect. It is the viewer who must be pleased. Spaces were designed not only to be practical and useful, but to be enjoyed.

Every era or culture has its obsessions: ours will probably be reported by future generations to have been that of gadgetry and electronics. Rome had its involvement with the arch; Byzantium experimented with domes; the Middle Ages struggled with the vaulting of heights; the Renaissance fell in love with *perspective*.

Before the Renaissance era artists and builders had been aware intuitively that objects at a distance were seen as smaller than those in the foreground, and this awareness was shown in their drawings. However, the Renaissance is credited with the "discovery" of perspective, because perspective was developed then as a geometric principle and an optical theory, and it established *mathematically* the relative dimensions of objects in three-dimensional space. Applied to painting, this meant that every element within the frame combined to create an atmosphere of depth and reality; buildings were created to give the viewer the same

*Bates Lowry. *Renaissance Architecture.* New York: George Braziller, 1971.

totality and to impress him, just as if he were viewing a picture.

Because Plato believed in a geometrical form of the universe, and Aristotle regarded the whole heaven as a numerical scale, Renaissance architect-theorists, who were enchanted by all the ideas of the classical period, arrived at the opinion that churches based on classic geometric axioms would be microcosms of the universe of God. The picture-story domes and the aspiring heights gave way to rational, balanced plans meant to mirror a universe that could be grasped and understood.

Thus the character and plans of churches began to change from those of the past. On the horizon, spires and towers of the Gothic were no longer multiplying; domes, reminiscent of the Romans, reappeared. These domes, however, differed from the Byzantine in which religious significance made the dome *the* central and most important feature of the church, dominating and determining both exterior and interior space. The Renaissance domes, even the most spectacular ones, were, by comparison, merely one architectural element in a composition planned as a totality.

Perhaps the best way to capture the flavor of the early Renaissance is to retell a story: how the cupola of the church of Santa Maria del Fiore in Florence was raised at the very beginning of the Italian Renaissance. The story has been recounted many times as an example of Renaissance experimentation, not only in plans and designs of buildings, but also in new, untried, more modern personal and political relationships between architects and patrons.

Just as with individuals in any other age, people of the Renaissance were competitive, jealous, prone to favoritism, indecision, disagreement, economic wariness, intrigue, and stratagems. This is made apparent by the original raconteur, Giorgio Vasari, in his fascinating account of Filippo

Brunelleschi,* the architect who carried on what might be considered the most successful one-man sick leave in history.

According to Vasari, Brunelleschi was a young Florentine architect-sculptor, unusually inventive, ingenious, and independent of spirit. He was well-educated in the manner of the times, having been apprenticed first to a goldsmith, then having had lessons in geometry, the Scriptures, and the writings of Dante. In his own studies of ancient buildings he spent much time in Rome, examining and measuring the ruins. Like every other artist of Florence, Brunelleschi hoped to solve the problem of raising the dome of a famous local church, Santa Maria del Fiore. The original architect, Arnolfo di Cambio, had died in the 1300s, leaving a wooden model with few clues as to his plans for the dome. Since that time, no one had had the courage to attempt to construct and raise to the required height a dome with a span to cover 138 feet. But Brunelleschi had studied the problem and was convinced he had a plan that would work. In 1407 the Warden of Works of the church and the Consuls of the Wool Guild decided they had enough money to think about finishing the church. When they called together the local artists, architects, and engineers to discuss raising the cupola, Brunelleschi was ready with his ideas. His plan seemed so simple compared with most of the others and was at the same time so original that the committee was wary of it. At meeting after meeting, Brunelleschi presented the same plan and attempted to explain it to the Consuls of the Wool Guild, who were untrained in technical matters. The other artists wasted no time in pointing out what they considered to be weak points in Brunelleschi's plan and presented plans of their own. Some strange and diverse solutions were sug-

*Giorgio Vasari. *Lives of the Artists*. Trans. George Bull. Baltimore: Penguin Books, 1965. Rev. ed. 1971.

gested. Some wanted to make the cupola out of pumice stone so that it would be less heavy; some even suggested that the best method would be to fill it with a mixture of earth and coins, so that when it was raised from the new level, those who wanted to could help themselves to the earth (for the coins) and so remove the earth without expense, leaving the dome standing. There were others who gave more technically competent advice, but no one except Brunelleschi had, in the long run, a confident plan.

Brunelleschi had made a model, but he was reluctant to show it. He was afraid that, with the committee members leaning first toward one idea, then another, the model could be studied but the project turned over to someone else.

It took thirteen years of discussions, indecision, and continued consultations — not only with local architects, but with architects invited to Florence from all over Europe — before Brunelleschi was finally offered the commission.

At once there was criticism and resentment among local officials. Much as in modern-day affairs, one faction protested the decision, saying it was too hasty (despite the thirteen years of discussion); another faction felt that a project of that size should not be in the hands of one person; and still another faction complained that Brunelleschi was too young. It was therefore decided, without consulting Brunelleschi, to give him a partner.

The man chosen was Lorenzo Ghiberti, an artist-sculptor at that time at the height of his fame because of the sculptured bronze doors he had just completed for the Baptistery of San Giovanni in Florence. But Brunelleschi was bitter about the partnership, because Ghiberti, basically a sculptor, understood nothing of Brunelleschi's highly original concept and apparently showed no evidence of wanting to learn. We can imagine Ghiberti appearing at the project occasionally, in his cloak and with his cane. We can see him walking around the site, pointing with his cane, commenting a few times with an ambiguous "Hmm," and an inexplicable "Ah!," and promptly leaving, whereas we know that Brunelleschi was at the site every day, giving all the orders, watching and helping with the work.

He superintended every detail, going himself to the lime ovens, checking the mixture of lime and sand for the mortar, ensuring that every brick was well baked, every stone sound and cut to size. Consulted about an awkward joint or turning, Brunelleschi would pick up a turnip and in that cut a model of how the job should be done . . . . He invented a new kind of barge to bring the marble . . . . He designed a mechanical hoist for raising heavy blocks, and a special kind of grappling iron. For this invention [he was reimbursed] for expenses in making it. These included wheels, pulleys, beams, balances, chains, rope, leather, yokes for the oxen working it, and 14 pails of glue.*

The final straw for Brunelleschi came when he heard even some of his friends claim that Ghiberti was equally responsible for the design of the new dome. He was infuriated. With the dome halfway raised, Brunelleschi bandaged his head, took to his bed, and let it be known that he was too ill to continue to go to the site.

Work stopped; confusion reigned; the masons stood around waiting to be told what to do next. Whenever a worried committeeman called on Brunelleschi to ask what was to be done, he simply held his head and said, "There's Ghiberti. Let him do something."

Ghiberti, however, was unable to give any clear instructions, so Brunelleschi's ploy worked well and rather quickly. Masons were paid even if they waited for instructions, just as they are today. And so it wasn't long before a subdued committee persuaded Brunelleschi to recover and

*Vincent Cronin. *The Florentine Renaissance*. New York: E. P. Dutton & Co., 1967.

*The dome of Santa Maria del Fiore. When the Consuls of the Wool Guild complained, "Lorenzo can do nothing without you," Brunelleschi replied, "But I can do perfectly well without Lorenzo."*

return to the site. Eventually all authority was left in Brunelleschi's hands, and the extraordinary accomplishment was recognized by scholars and historians of the time as his alone. The fact that the dome had been conceived by one man and executed under his direction against all odds marked a turning point in the Middle Ages' view of the architect. It gave back to the word "inventor" its proper meaning, for in the commission papers Brunelleschi is named *inventore* — the originator. And Vincent Cronin tells us that the dome became such a beloved city symbol that "Florentines abroad, instead of saying they were homesick, said they were 'sick for the dome.' "

# Renaissance and Rebellion

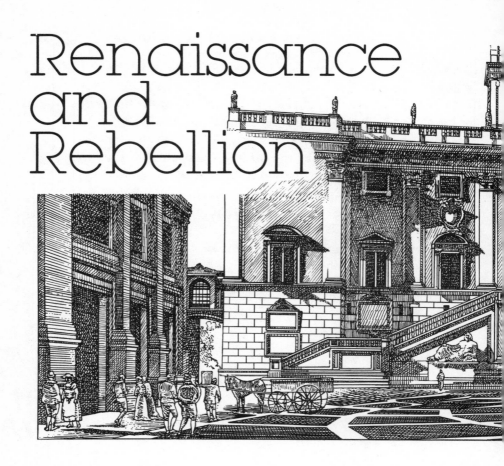

The architects of the Renaissance period earned the respect that was given them. They were hard-working, extraordinarily well-rounded, and distinguished in several arts. The famous were usually painters or sculptors as well as architects; one, Sir Christopher Wren, the seventeenth-century English architect, was first a celebrated mathematician and professor of astronomy. Now his fame lives on in some fifty-two London churches, St. Paul's Cathedral, and many secular buildings at Oxford and Cambridge universities.

Usually an architect had considerable knowledge of mechanical parts and could design clocks or war machines;

142

*Palazzo del Senatore (The Campidoglio, Rome)*

he might also in the course of his training have learned to
make surgical instruments. When we use the term "Renaissance Man" today, we mean someone who resembles in his
diverse abilities those artists of the fifteenth to eighteenth
centuries who were talented and skilled in many areas of the
arts.

Italian Renaissance architects were often called to other
countries to counsel the architects in the royal courts there.
In time, all the European countries began to produce men
who were brilliant in the arts, and the early Italianate influence was supplanted by national themes and variations.

In France, where a Renaissance began between the six-

143

teenth and seventeenth centuries, we find monuments such as the Palais du Louvre and Versailles and the great châteaux, and in England churches and buildings in architectural styles known there as Elizabethan, Jacobean, Stuart, and Georgian — names taken from the ruling families of the time. In America the American Renaissance style can be seen in Independence Hall and Mount Vernon, in William and Mary College in Virginia, and it can be recognized as an influence on some of the buildings along Fifth Avenue and in other areas of New York City.

During the Renaissance architects worked predominantly on churches, church buildings, palaces, public buildings, fortifications, and grand plans for royalty and other noble personages. Those buildings that still stand are a reminder of a wealthy world, and they tell us much about the rich, the powerful, and the talented of the times, but little about the growing middle class and the poor. That story is more likely to be found in what is left of the old cities.

There is an ambiguous note about the Renaissance. On one hand are our liberal views, which object to the oppression and domination of the individual person; many of our social ideals; our awareness that living spaces need to meet different and varied practical and psychological needs and tastes — all these can be traced to beginnings in fifteenth- and sixteenth-century philosophic thought. This thought is reflected in the architectural treatises of that time, with their emphasis on human values, and their attempts to establish laws, principles, and ideals for those who build, not for gods or for the State or out of religious fervor, but, simply, for other men.

On the other hand, there was a concentration of power in the royal courts of Europe and in the Popes and Papal Court, matched only by the autocracy of ancient empires. While not so bloodthirsty in action, this power base not

*An Italian villa in the classical tradition, which influenced much
subsequent English and early American Renaissance architecture.*

only maintained a society of hierarchies but was an influence against simplicity. It helped bring about the final
phase of Renaissance style, a full-scale reaction against
the classic disciplines, called *Baroque*.

Michelangelo died in 1564, at the age of eighty-nine.
During his long lifetime architecture had changed in degree but not in basic style. The absolute devotion to classic disciplines — scale, proportion, and rules — which had
been an essential part of early Renaissance design gradually gave way to the urgencies of imagination and self-

expression and to the desire to evoke an emotional response in the viewer. With the exception of a few ardent
adherents to the academic classical, architects became
more and more fascinated with the illusionary possibilities of perspective and the drama of the unexpected,
as against the rational and disciplined.

Theater is a good example of what is meant by the
illusionary possibilities of perspective. We already know
that in ancient Greece the theater was outdoors, built into
or carved out of an undulating, hilly natural arena space,
and that in Roman days the theater moved indoors, developed structured tiers of seats, the curtain, and a fairly
impressive stage with niches and statuary. This gave a
backdrop with an impression of scenery, but in the Renaissance the modern illusionary effect of three-
dimensional scenery began to develop. Lanes cut through
the stage backdrop were narrowed from front to back to

*Note the illusion of space created by the use of perspective in this*
*theater scenery of the Renaissance period.*

give the illusion of roads, and all the effects of sky, horizon, buildings, and depth, so familiar today, were begun at this time.

More important, what was happening on the stage in experiments with perspective was the same sort of experimentation that was going on in the design of facades and interiors of buildings. Effects were achieved by using all kinds of decorative elements — columns, cornices, balustrades, paintings, carving, and sculpture.

Exteriors, too, were planned to reflect a plan in perspec-

*The placement of buildings to contain and make pleasurable outdoor public spaces, and the use of colonnades in outdoor squares were a major concern of Renaissance architects.*

tive: courts, squares, stairways, walks, buildings, wherever possible, were designed as a composition in a setting. Shakespeare, who wrote, "All the world's a stage . . ." during Renaissance years, anticipated the Baroque landscape of the seventeenth and eighteenth centuries perfectly. The city planning was, above all, a dramatic and three-dimensional theatrical setting, creating living backdrops for royal elegance and church panoply.

Just as the Renaissance was a time of competition and conflicts between artists and patrons, it was also a time for conflicts among nations, and these often led, in the latter part of the Renaissance, to wars. During the seventeenth century there was the Thirty Years' War (1618-1648); the Puritan Revolution of 1642 in England, and constant religious conflict which came to a head in the Reformation and the Counter-Reformation. It was a century of discovery, geographical and scientific. The world continued to widen fast. It was both rich, restless, and excessive; poor, wretched, and fanatical. It is not surprising that architecture, too, eventually began to break with the past — distort, alter, and remodel old forms. The bonds of classic discipline broke completely when most Renaissance architecture after Michelangelo exploded into the Baroque. The Baroque architect threw away the rule book, the classic measurements, restraints, and all the precepts.

Flat facades began to curve outward; classical square and rectangular spaces in the hands of the Italians Francesco Borromini (1599-1667) and Giovanni Lorenzo Bernini (1598-1680) became a series of interrelated rounds and ovals. The oval was the new plaything; today it always spells Baroque. We find an early mid-1500s example, looking somewhat like a large oval casserole, forming the shape of the dome of one of the Sant' Andrea churches in Rome. The church is otherwise a rectangular form designed by Giacomo da Vignola. A more famous church, Sant' Andrea al Quirinale, by Bernini, also in Rome, is itself an oval form.

Baroque architects kept many classic forms, playing with them in a kind of creative take-over. In Paris the Church of the Invalides, with its three-tiered dome, and the Panthéon (Sainte Geneviève), with its circular spaces inside squared arms and its classic porch, are considered Baroque, but are obviously made up of many classical elements.

Baroque at its height represented self-expression gone wild. *Pediments* (the triangular form used over windows and doors in classic design), cornices, *entablatures* (beams), moldings, and columns were twisted, broken, reformed, duplicated, and decorated in later Baroque (called *Rococo*) with carved statues of saints, angels, and especially cherubs. These prolific denizens of Rococo-Baroque are poised on every pedestal, peer from every cornice, and hover like birds from heaven on swooping, curving moldings, a world removed from the pure, straight lines of the classic forms. We see this later phase of the Baroque in the Abbey Church in Zwiefalten, Germany, and also, in southern Germany, in Vierzehnheiligen, we see a grand flourish of the oval shape in the linked spaces of the interior plan of the Pilgrimage Church. It is obvious that these buildings were not designed to be comprehended intellectually. All interior space, in scale, which was grandiose, in dramatic effects of light and shadow, and in unexpected and often overwhelming decoration, was concentrated on producing a sensational emotional effect.

This was especially true of churches. In a divided Catholic and Protestant world, catechism, salvation, and religious exultation became of greater personal concern, less community oriented. Royal and well-to-do individuals showed a preference for private chapel spaces, private prayers, and

*The staircases of the Renaissance were theatrical backgrounds for pomp, ceremony, beautiful gowns, and formal entrances.*

sought close advisory relationships with the clergy. Indulgences were beseeched, donations given, personal repentances suffered, and the interiors of Baroque churches provided an extravagant background for these personal dramas.

In the secular world nations were coalescing around central royal power. The royal courts were wealthy, and the court ministers and followers considered themselves worldly gentlemen with a taste for style and elegance. Excess in taste was not frowned upon so much as was lack of taste. And as the gap between rich and poor widened, excess became increasingly stylish. European royalty — with the exception of Henry IV of France, whose concern for the common man and whose social reforms ended when he was assassinated by a religious fanatic early in the seventeenth century — concentrated on beautifying cities and on setting the stage for royal affairs, entrances, and exits, while ignoring social programs for bettering the lot of the poor. Such policies gave us some beautiful buildings but did nothing to solve the problems of slums. The seventeenth and eighteenth centuries produced the great city squares and sculptured fountains of Italy, the Versailles of France, the vistas of Paris, and some of the best and loveliest open spaces and choicest secular buildings throughout Europe. The staircase, indoors and outdoors, became important and gained new magnificence. Wide, curving, a three-dimensional sculpture, with people at different levels in fashionable silks and satins — it, too, was drama of the first order.

Baroque has been called "space in action," so it fitted a century of action and conflict. At its best, Baroque was various, dramatic, daring, and full of fantasy. At its worst, it was disorder and, finally, in some cases, embellishment to the point of the absurd or grotesque. Like any rebellion, it seems to have consisted of freedom, reform, distortion, and

*The grandiose decoration of Baroque at its height swept throughout Europe in the last phase of Renaissance building. Germany and Austria were particularly infatuated with the ornamental possibilities, which sometimes were carried to improbable extremes.*

excess, all bound together, creating an impact which, whether appealing or distasteful, is impossible to ignore. It defines a world of excitement and searchings, but also conflict and anxiety, and it predates the coming political and industrial revolutions of the eighteenth and nineteenth centuries.

# Exterior Spaces: The Shapes of Towns and Cities

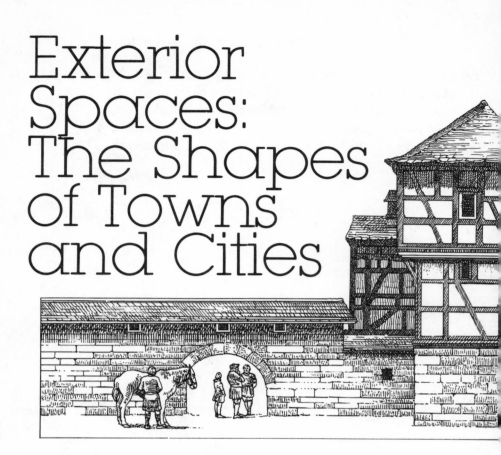

H eight seems to have been an obsession with human beings ever since the primitive communes of pre-history raised their monolithic stones by methods we can only speculate upon and in patterns and for reasons we have yet to fathom.

In the case of the cathedrals, and, earlier on, the ziggurats of the Mesopotamian valley, height was the result of religious beliefs, but more often it has come about in answer to pressures for expansion. Wherever large numbers of people crowded together, either to live behind walls for protection or to be near transportation and trade; wherever horizontal expansion had its limitations, the alternate solution was to

154

*Medieval street scene*

go up. This was the solution that brought about the *insulae*, or apartment blocks in Rome; the tall, narrow houses on the crowded streets of medieval towns; and, combined with technical advances, such as the invention of the elevator, the multistoried buildings of the modern city. So it is possible to think of a city — that three-dimensional, live, ever-changing organism created by people out of a need to have a permanent base where they can live, socialize, and trade with their fellows — as both a vertical and horizontal penetration of space.

For the serf of medieval times, the merchant, or the tradesman, the city meant a kind of freedom, but to the

155

nomad the city was a prison, a blight. It was there to be
demolished and plundered. And throughout early history
demolished it was, on a grand scale. To become a slave, as a
prisoner of war, was, perhaps, the kindest fate a defeated
city dweller could hope for; other alternatives were rape,
torture, the torch, beheading, flaying, crushing by ele-
phants, and other gruesome acts of hatred and revenge
by the conquerers of a city. Nothing, apparently, was too
horrible to inflict on defeated city dwellers. Often the cities
themselves were burned to the ground, while the nomad
conquerers, refusing to live within the gates, pitched their
tents outside. And yet even some of these razed cities came
back, were revitalized many years later to become powerful
again.

It was this concentration of power and wealth that chal-
lenged not only the nomads but the kings and emperors who
wished to enlarge their territories. Conquer the city and you
conquered the civilization that created it. The next step
depended on the conqueror. Either he established a new city
built upon the ruins of the old, or he moved the city and
citizens who were left to a spot more to his liking, or he
incorporated some of the old into some of the new. Some
ancient conquerors moved people around like pawns. Wish-
ing to change a site, the king or emperor might even divert a
river, changing its course so that the center of trade would
be shifted to a different and, from his point of view, more
acceptable spot.

Many of the earliest ancient cities had their beginnings as
fortified entities at the crossroads of trade routes, a river
mouth, a seaport, a land route for salt, spices, obsidian,
gold, or other metals. *Site* was important — a place where
water was available, defense possible, and where transportation in or out could be secured.

In an agrarian economy the city dweller was a new and
different person, one who ate without having to grow and

harvest his own food. Communities grew up out of farmers' surpluses — some started only as bartering centers — and townspeople became dependent on one another's trades and skills. In ancient times cities attracted the craftsmen, artists, merchants, scribes, garrison soldiers, and priests. The city was the nucleus of culture and cults, a setting for displays of power, royal or religious, as well as for marketplaces and for defense alliances.

In the growing city-towns of the ancients, streets were simply viewed as spaces between buildings; as passageways, they ran helter-skelter and were narrow, crooked, and dirty. Nebuchadnezzar, with his liking for pomp and ceremony, introduced the idea of a wide street down which great processions could march. In Babylon, at least, several such streets were created, and the Babylonians gave the same kind of attention to their construction as they gave to the buildings of temples and palaces; each of these streets was named for a god. With the exception of the old, winding streets of the Middle Ages, streets became important planned elements of a city, developing and changing in accordance with the latest transportation technology: the invention of the cart, the domestication of the camel (which brought caravans and large animals within city limits), the use of wider chariots, the speed of the automobile, or the traffic of streetcars, trucks, and buses.

Pressures or advances brought about by *technology* change not only the width, direction, and contours of the streets, but the characters of all cities. Horse-drawn chariots, for example, were one of the technological pressures that radically changed the shape and contour of ancient city-towns, just as automobiles continue to change our cities today. The need to widen the streets to accommodate the chariot was only the beginning of greater changes affecting an entire city. The horses had to be fed and cared for and checked for disease; the chariots and their accessories had to be maintained. The contour of the ground on which chariots could travel was also a big problem, because corners are a difficult turn for chariot wheels to make. Consequently long straight streets or large oval-shaped roadways were preferred and introduced. Other considerations were how to handle the addition of the chariot to the heavy traffic of carts and other wheeled vehicles in busy streets already thick with people and with oxen and donkeys transporting goods.

Perhaps there were even problems concerning how to take care of and hospitalize those who were knocked over by these "wild" machines. There was certainly a parking problem, although apparently it was dealt with summarily, from our point of view, early in its appearance. In Assyria it was not the vehicle that was towed away; it was the driver. "Sennacherib, the Assyrian engineer-king, set up the first no-parking signs. He placed posts along the processional way in Nineveh, inscribed: ROYAL ROAD. LET NO MAN LESSEN IT. Not yet satisfied, Sennacherib decreed that any scoundrel who parked a chariot or other vehicle should be slain and his body impaled on a stake before his house."* Thus, the chariot introduced not only a whole new way of life (and punishment), but because it was the cause of so many changes in the city's physical form, it is considered a basic element in changing the Roman military camp format to the more complex shape of a fortified city-town.

Every wall built seemed to have been a new challenge to an enemy determined to pull it down with siege tools, knock it down with battering rams, or blow it up by digging and crawling beneath to mine it in secret. From time to time new walls, always stronger, thicker, and deeper, took the place of the old, and the city within and the shape without changed

*L. Sprague De Camp. *The Ancient Engineers*. Garden City, N.Y.: Doubleday & Co., Inc., 1963.

*Walls shaped ancient cities and those of the Middle Ages by limiting boundary lines, but they were a necessary protection against attack and plunder. A city's site was enhanced if, like Mont-Saint-Michel, it also rose atop a seemingly impregnable mountain peak.*

again. When it was discovered that raiders attacking with picks could not be seen at the corners of a square, and that sappers bent on undermining the walls were out of reach of arrows at those corners, the square tower became obsolete, and the round tower replaced it.

For thousands of years walls were a great influence on the shapes of cities. They restricted a city's growth outward; as a result the inner land became both precious and crowded. Eventually buildings had to go vertical, and streets remained narrow. Even after walls lost most of their technical advantage as defense, particularly when cannon appeared, they remained psychologically important to the townspeople's sense of security.

Defense was always of primary importance, but ideas of how to achieve it changed, and this, too, (a combination of the influences *people* and *technology*), had an effect on the character of the city. The concern with defense led to the need for a powerful, prestigious central authority able to deal with other powerful rulers to make alliances that could keep the city safe. This created behind the city walls a center, sometimes with inner walls of its own. In early civilizations the center was a fortress-like building, a citadel, built on the highest ground and housing the ruling authorities. It also served as a refuge for the townspeople in times of trouble. In some cultures the center was composed of buildings that surrounded a main structure devoted to the gods — a temple, or a palace in which the king was also a priest or played a primary role in the society's religious beliefs. The Romans centered their city around the buildings of state. The emerging cities of the Middle Ages almost always surrounded the Church, which became increasingly the symbol of power and authority, and this central core became the most significant characteristic of all medieval cities and was the dominant factor in determining their shapes.

Most changes in cities can be attributed to *technology* and to the ways people have reacted and adapted to the new problems and pressures that resulted from technological innovation. Sailing ships brought about thriving port cities, and steam locomotives made possible the establishment of inland centers, towns that grew into cities, such as Chicago and St. Louis in America's Midwest. Elevators made six-story buildings seem provincial and afforded vertical space for thousands more in an urban area. Again, the character of cities changed radically.

The automobile brought about new pressures, new needs. In all its forms, from private cars to trucks, it has completely altered the look of town and cityscape and the rhythm of people's lives. It has radically changed the methods of delivery of foods and goods within cities; it has made possible great transient travel and individual movement, resulting in the dispersement of traditional centers; it has necessitated new types of indoor and outdoor structures and spaces — the home garage, the parking garage, the parking lot, the pedestrian mall — and has affected the aspect of street spaces in the city. Its widespread use has reduced the importance of railroads, and, as a result, arrested the growth of or blotted out many cities which owed their existence to station stops. The automobile has created instead many diverse suburban areas, which have made towns and cities primarily business cores, the centers for ever-widening areas of surrounding countryside.

The airplane is another technological advance that has had an enormous influence on city life. By supplanting shipping for the carrying of most goods, planes have sounded an economic death knell for many ports. Their fast transportation has made available all over the world the same materials, technical advice, and mechanical inventions. In so doing, planes have made possible on every continent an international type of city in which only the older sections retain the flavor of a particular country or civilization. The new-city areas are very similar to one another, with their skyscrapers, streets, lighting, density of traffic, and civic operations.

The airplane, even more than the automobile, has affected the rhythm of people's lives and particularly the time element in their ways of doing business. It has changed the flow and mix of residents, businesses, and transient travel within the confines of the city, and it has given large cities a crowded, active, and restless atmosphere, and towns a commercial appearance and erratic growth patterns.

These examples show how some technological discoveries have created pressures for change in a city, but more important for the city dweller to understand is the fact that technological discoveries *always* create pressures for change in a city. The technological invention need not even be of a structural nature but can be as far-fetched as the horse-collar. As Wolf Schneider says:

> An important advance was made in the eleventh century when the horse-collar made wagon transportation of tremendous loads feasible. The old-style breast harness allowed the horse to pull only with its breastbone; the leather girth pressed the shoulder blades together and inhibited breathing. The horse-collar made it possible to utilize fully the horse's pulling power by putting the strain squarely on the horse's powerful shoulders, without pressing on the lungs. This invention, by facilitating the transportation of heavy loads overland, made it possible for inland cities, as well as those on seacoast or riverbank, to become important trading centers.*

The horse-collar happened a long time ago, but a more

*Wolf Schneider. *Babylon Is Everywhere: The City as Man's Fate.* New York: McGraw-Hill Book Co., 1963.

modern invention equally unrelated directly to structure — perhaps a small electronic device or beamed heat
from satellite solar stations — will prove to us once again
that, despite nostalgic hopes, a city can never go back
to the way it was. It either dies because it is no longer active
or useful, or it changes its character, sometimes in small
ways, sometimes definitively. But it is *never* static.

Although many towns grow to city size, there is no au-
tomatic progression from village to town to city. Many villages and towns remain particularized entities — a fishing
village, a rural marketplace, a mining town, a manufactur-
ing town, a town of hatmakers, clockmakers, rug weavers,
or tool-and-die machinists. Each retains its own atmosphere, but a town and city may share on a different scale
a similar underlying design layout. These town and city
plans have various origins, many going back to ancient
times.

Common to Europe are the shapes of towns that developed from some of the many jumbled, unplanned settlements of the pre-Roman European landscape — *castra*, from
which we get the suffix "chester." A map of England reveals
many "chesters" (Winchester, Manchester), and the colonists brought the suffix to the New World. In the eleventh
century the prototype fortified medieval town made its appearance and introduced the "burg" (sometimes "berg"),
home of the merchant citizen of the Middle Ages, the
"burgher."

Another prototype layout for cities is more common in the
United States. It is called the *grid*, and is the underlying
principle of organization for many modern cities and towns,
notably New York City and many midwestern towns. The
grid system (streets running north-south, crossing east-
west) is the easiest and quickest way to lay out a new city,
provided the land is flat. Hill towns must follow contours,

but the flat plains of mid-America lent themselves perfectly to the grid when the railroad moved westward and settlers were in a hurry to establish new towns.

The grid system comes from antiquity. The origin of the principle is uncertain, but it was consistently used by the Romans, who laid out their military camps in this way, regardless of where they were located in the growing Empire. The Roman camps hardly varied from this orderly and practical arrangement, whether the armies expected a short stay or a long occupation. As it turned out, some of the

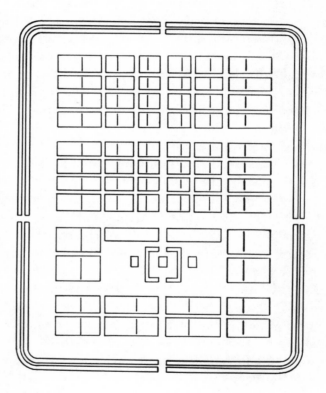

*Layout of a Roman camp, showing the ordered north-south, east-west plan —easy and quick to measure and lay out, practical for movement of people and goods.*

occupations lasted hundreds of years, and when these original campsites became sites of towns, the grid laid out remained the basic design plan.

The Romans were also the originators of the idea of a capital city that would serve as a symbol representing in those days an empire, in these days a nation. The capital city was made up of all those kinds of buildings familiar to a city today: town dwellings (then palaces or villas), theaters, churches (then temples), tenements, libraries, sports arenas, gymnasiums (then public baths), civic buildings, and outdoor courtyards and parks. In Africa, in Gaul, in Britain, when the Romans built, their first priority was to erect buildings and monuments that would link the provincial city spiritually and politically with the mother city, Rome. A forum, a senate, temples and a theater, usually public baths and an arena were placed in about the same relationship to each other in as close a copy as possible of the home buildings. Romans spread all these city elements in an organized way throughout the Empire, establishing provincial cities that were like smaller prints of an original painting. So we see today, in such diverse areas as Africa, Sicily, Britain, and France (Gaul), remains of similar layouts in town design.

Long after the end of the Roman Empire, completely different kinds of towns appeared in Europe and grew to considerable numbers in the eleventh century. About two hundred years earlier the movement toward community living and away from serfdom centering around the feudal knight or the Church had its beginning when people began fortifying their villages instead of relying entirely on the lord's castle for protection. Many other medieval cities grew out of the early tangle of crooked alleys which themselves had grown up surrounding monasteries and early universities.

A town gradually came to be defined as a place where

many people had built their houses and kept their shops and storehouses, made rules and laws about how they would live, and protected those who came to work and live there. (By the twelfth century towns were strong enough in themselves to resist demands for return of serfs who had left their masters' lands. A former master had to sue for extradition.)

All these towns were noted for their lack of sanitation and for the constant exposure to the hazards of fire and disease. The colorful, mythic, transitional eras of the Middle Ages, with their barely discernible undercurrents of the scientific and humanist thinking that was to come, were without any of the comforts of the Romans of ancient times or those of today. An open drain ran down the middle of most streets. The roads, most of them unpaved, were muddy in wet weather, and clouds of dust when the weather was dry. Refuse thrown to the streets from windows was a common practice. The houses — wooden skeletons filled with rubble plastered over — were high and narrow, pressed close together across narrow, winding streets. They usually contained the merchant's storehouse or shop as well as his family's living quarters.

At the same time, most early European towns were harmonious in appearance. The layout of streets and squares followed closely the demands of the natural resources of the site, and materials indigenous to the surrounding countryside were used for building the houses, since they were most easily available. The result was a blend and unity of structure, color, and texture seldom seen in a modern town or city. And the Middle Ages loved color. The few old gray buildings still existing from Gothic times in the unreconstructed older sections of some European cities were once painted in brilliant reds and blues. Bright signboards and banners hung from taverns and inns, and there was gold glowing in the coats of arms marking the finer houses of the nobility.

During the Middle Ages the nucleus of the town was the
Church. Since it was there one could find those relatively
few people who could read and write, townspeople came not
only to worship but to turn over their deeds of property for
safekeeping. Arms were stored there for emergencies, and in
peaceful times the Church was the center for social life, its
spaces turned into a large dining hall during a festival, or its
facade a background for markets and, sometimes, miracle
plays. There were no theater buildings in the towns of the
Middle Ages.

*Plan of a typical cellular city of the Middle Ages. Church
buildings formed the center or nucleus.*

"Nucleus" is a good word to describe such a center, because the medieval town had, in its circular form, a cellular character and greatly resembled in growth as well as looks a complex biological organism of many interlocking elements. Towns grew from the center outward, piece by piece, until halted and pushed inward on themselves by the fortified walls at the perimeter. Crowds and congestion were a common problem. Though new outer walls were often considered and sometimes built, they were expensive and took years of labor. As towns grew into cities and people again filled all available space, land speculators thrived and rents increased three- and fourfold, while within the walls the great concerns after defense were water supply, fire, sanitation problems, disease, smell, and thievery, probably in that order.

The medieval town, because it was an essential element in and an outgrowth of a newly developing society of landowners, shopkeepers, and potentially powerful families of wealth, contained the seeds of a new political power quite different from that of the ancient city-towns. Not only were the highborn or wealthy individuals influential, but the craftsmen's guilds developed into increasingly powerful influences on society, as did the average town dweller with his propensity for popular protest and revolutionary ideas. Kings and emperors needed cities, but at the same time they feared them — their wealth, their energy, and their uncontrollable population. It was in the towns and cities that the modern concept of democracy developed.

The period during which Renaissance thinking was at its height, the sixteenth through the eighteenth centuries, gradually transformed the medieval city, and much of the planning at that time provided many of the familiar details and the more attractive aspects of our modern cities.

A 1783 ruling [in Paris] prohibited the opening of streets less than 33 ft. wide and the building of houses

more than 66 ft. high. The appearance of the streets
changed: signs with street names appeared in 1729, oil
street-lamps in 1757, and in 1762 shop signs were
placed flat on the facades to facilitate night illumina-
tion. Shop-front windows became common. Following
London's example, sidewalks appeared in 1782 in the
[present] Place de l'Odéon. The numbering of houses
was first instituted in the suburbs in 1728 to prevent
new building; it spread through Paris sporadically after
1780. The principal sanitation efforts were directed at
the cemeteries . . . whose fumes began to be hazardous.
They were all emptied and closed.*

Politically, the entity of "town" was ripe for change during these eras. Any town that became a city had become
more powerful in the process. It was now the core of organized society. Some cities were almost independent states,
subject only to a king, and, if Roman Catholic, the king and
the Pope. Cities were rich, or, rather, the rich in the cities
were very rich. Town planning focused not on improving
living conditions for the common man but on making all
that surrounded a person more beautiful. The Renaissance
obsession with perspective was responsible not only for
matchless vistas, exquisite landscapes of fountains and gardens, large squares or piazzas accented by statuary of correct and considered scale or graced by public fountains, but,
in general, for the proportioned beauty achieved by artfully
arranged compositions relating buildings to each other and
to outdoor spaces, gardens, and squares. The same concern
with symmetry, proportion, and perspective given to interior spaces at this time was carried outdoors.

Those architectural treatises of the fifteenth, sixteenth,
and seventeenth centuries that were full of philosophical
thought about individuals and humanity also abounded in

*Pierre Couperie. *Paris Through the Ages*. New York: George Braziller,
1971. Trans. from *Paris au fil du temps*. Cuénot, 1968.

theories about "ideal" cities, their geometric structure, their functions and internal relationships. In practice, however, the emphasis was not on social improvements; rather, buildings were looked upon as part of an over-all composition — three-dimensional stage settings for people to move about in and enjoy looking at, with the outdoor squares, perhaps, to serve as social meeting places. The result was the opening up of new streets and the widening of squares, partly because of wheeled carriages and traffic and possible royal processions, and partly because of the very real threat of narrow, winding streets as breeding places for plots against powerful princes. However, it seems that many of these improvements took place simply because of the great desire during these centuries to achieve beauty.

In the later Baroque period of the Renaissance, motion of all kinds began to fascinate the architect-planners. They were particularly interested in the motion of water; consequently, fountains became even more ornamental and important. Motion through space was embodied for them in the movement and design of staircases. Stairs had once been considered merely necessary nuisances, built almost like vertical tunnels just wide enough to get from one level to another, but they had developed during early Renaissance times to graceful and decorative elements. Now, in the Baroque period, they became elaborate, and one can almost imagine the architects exploring space with their twists and turns and graceful inclines. Staircases were brought outdoors, too, during these centuries, and became part of the new civic spaces.

Another concern of the Renaissance years had to do with the reorganization of city defense lines. The whole idea of fortification had changed so radically with new methods of warfare that designing effective walls had become an increasingly complex project, and a trained sense of engineering was necessary to analyze the slants, angles, and special undulating contours of not just one wall but walls within walls. No longer did the aggressor in a siege on a city move in close to scale or undermine a wall; no longer could the defender pour boiling oil or reach the opposite army with arrows from the ramparts. Now warfare was carried on with distance between the two armies. Towers disappeared, and the total plan of city defense was turned over to those experts of the Renaissance eras, the architect-engineers. As a result, the same artists who created the churches, palaces, and civic areas (among them, Leonardo da Vinci and Michelangelo) were called upon to design and engineer not only fortifications but the harbor works of those times as well. (Harbor works had always been exceedingly important to a city's life. In ancient days, before adequate dredging machines and methods were developed, a harbor filling with silt meant the decline and end of many a port city.)

Silted harbors and devastation by siege or by war were only two of the several destroyers of cities. The decline of a city is as telling, if not as happy, as its growth. Natural causes — earthquakes, fires, and floods — were always effective in razing large areas. On the other hand, the city dwellers of history have shown many gifts for survival, and one seems to be a remarkable ability to rebuild.

As we have seen, change in trading routes often meant the demise of one center and the birth of another; changing types of transportation meant the same; mining towns turned into desert wastes when the ore ran out, and industrial towns collapsed when a primary business or factory closed or moved. All these are fairly immediate, understandable death blows resulting from a single happening. There is another kind of disintegration and decline, however, an inner malaise, extending over a long period of time, exemplified by an account of the decline of ancient Rome, which has in fact a disturbing modern tone.

Rome, once a village, a little country town on the Tiber

River, became, as Roman conquests increased and the Empire grew, a place of centralized organization for a growing population, expanding commerce, and intensified interchange with the rest of the Mediterranean world. Its ability to assimilate different peoples and cultures gave it the necessary fluidity for the growth of a city. Its rise was a natural process, as was its fall, which, ironically, came about partly because of its greatness. The fall was a long process lasting more than two hundred years, in which the city's organization became so overworked, so unwieldy, so complex, that it began to overbalance and topple of its own weight. There was vast wealth and abject poverty and too many opportunities for the misuse of power. Poverty and disintegration, greed and luxury existed side by side. By the time the barbarian invasions watered down the spirit and essence of the city, the fall of Rome was already latent, and each new battle the outward event that made the reality of the death of the city more manifest.

Another kind of death — that of a familiar way of living in a city — takes place when technology causes such a drastic change in the quality of living that old established city patterns disintegrate and disappear. This happened, in the name of progress, with the coming of the nineteenth-century industrial city, which was catastrophic to the whole previous concept of town environment. The Industrial Revolution swept the countryside, scarred it with chimneys and coke ovens, curtained it with soot and smoke. It took over the rivers, churned and harnessed the waters for power, polluted the streams with chemical overflows. In the era of *laissez-faire*, expendiency and speed were the two most important influences altering the landscape.

In the nineteenth century the natural rhythms of life, the aesthetic concerns of the previous centuries, the relationship of town to landscape all disappeared. Industry and the machine made for haphazard development of towns as well as irresponsible abandonment of them according to factory or mining needs or the acumen of developers.

The Industrial Revolution also brought with it the necessity for new types of buildings never before envisioned: factories, railway stations, special warehouses, and so on. It also brought new building materials — cast iron and steel — and these two factors caused an enormous aesthetic confusion. At first no one knew how to build for this type of living. A new kind of city had been born, and it would have to struggle to find its own solutions.

# Skyscrapers and Schizophrenia

A t the beginning of the 1800s life was lived at a rather leisurely pace. The stagecoach was the chief means of transportation by land; sailing ships commanded the seas. Local materials and regional crafts characterized almost all building. Before the end of the century steam was propelling hundreds of different new machines, and European countries were producing such an excess of cheaply manufactured materials that new areas of the world were aggressively and frantically sought for colonization, chiefly because, from an economic point of view, they were needed to provide not only raw materials but

174

*The changing urban scene*

as return markets for surplus goods.

The century began, as far as architecture was concerned, with a continuation of the classic style and with the traditional aristocratic or court patron still in evidence as a client. It ended in a life style completely separated from the traditions of Renaissance Europe and in the disappearance of the noble patron and the appearance of a new client class oriented toward the economics of business. There came about a decline in the use of regional crafts, materials, and labor, but a great increase in the production of glass and metal, particularly iron and steel. The century began with

175

Renaissance-Baroque techniques of construction and ended with the first scientifically planned foundation work for skyscrapers.

The nineteenth century has been called a schizophrenic century, and with reason. Two dominant opposing trends were at work. The first, continuing from seeds planted in the eighteenth century, the aftermath of the "Liberty, Equality, Fraternity" theme of the French Revolution, and the "All Men Are Created Equal" theme of the American Revolution, was the voice of liberalism calling for social reform and universal education. Democratic and utopian theories abounded. There was confidence in reason and logic, delight in poetry and music, and belief in idealism as a way to a better life for all. This approach to living was almost buried beneath the avalanche of the Industrial Revolution.

The Industrial Revolution brought to the fore more exploitation of workers than thoughts for their pursuits of happiness, larger cities with the most crowded slums in history, the use of standardized products easier and cheaper to make and ship than regional crafts and the products of individuals, and entirely new kinds of buildings, both in purpose and manner of construction. It was a disparate influence leading to a split in nineteenth-century architecture. It put homes, certain important public buildings, and important churches into the category of art work, and these were felt, during most of the century, to be the concern of the architects, who were considered by the public to be primarily artists. On the other hand, the design and building of the business buildings, factories, railroad stations, housing (as opposed to "homes") for workers, and the large industrial plants and warehouses were taken over by the engineers. It made for confusion in the architects' realm since for the first time architecture was no longer supposed to deal with the basic realities and essentials of the new era. The result was, until the end of the century, a grand battle of styles, revivals by copy or modification of historic conventions: continuance, first, of the Renaissance classic; then a Gothic revival followed by a Greek revival; a period of Romanticism, the "Italian Villa," the "French Provincial," and the like; and eventually what has been termed eclecticism.

(*Eclecticism* is the taking of elements and details of past architectural styles and combining them into a new design for a building.)

At first glance the buildings that resulted seemed to have been influenced very little by *people* and the way they lived

*An extreme and amusing example of eclecticism, the Vedanta Society Temple in San Francisco manages to combine onion domes, medieval castle crenellation, and Moorish arches.*

then until one relates the split that took place in architecture to a similar split in society. The new client — the businessman, the manufacturer — found by day cheapness and practicality an ideal goal; in the evenings, at leisure at home, he expected to be led to "culture" — to reading, music, poetry, and art history — by the women of his family.

The average Victorian businessman lacked the kind of knowledge and background of art and architecture that was a traditional attribute of the aristocratic clients of the past. He was usually well-to-do and able to travel and be impressed by elegant architecture of the past; he followed with zeal the "battle of styles"; he read about "the dreaming spires," vied with his neighbors for a more imposing home, and at the same time had built under his direction horrendous factories and warehouses based on the *economical* use of standardized materials. It never occurred to him that the iron, steel, and glass used only in a utilitarian and inexpensive way could and would become in the next century, the twentieth, the architectural materials of the times.

The whole nature of architecture and the look of cities changed when iron and steel usurped the place of stone, wood, and brick as the most widely used structural materials for buildings.

In England the first proof that iron and glass could be used in an attractive and aesthetic way was a building known as the Crystal Palace, erected in London to house the Great Exhibition of 1851. It was designed by an extraordinarily talented man, Joseph Paxton (later Sir Joseph Paxton), a landscape gardener and estate manager, whose previous outstanding architectural accomplishment had been the building of an unusually large conservatory for the Duke of Devonshire.

Paxton was able to create for the Exhibition a long, spacious glass-and-iron prefabricated structure which from an engineering point of view would have been a singular tech-

*The Crystal Palace in its heyday, a great architectural*
*breakthrough in design and method of construction. It was*
*moved in 1854 to Sydenham, damaged by fire in the 1930s, then*
*demolished in 1941 so that it would not serve as a marker to*
*enemy air raiders.*

nical achievement even as a factory building, yet to the
amazement and delight of the thousands who eventually
visited there, it retained the ambience and charm of garden
greenhouses and orangeries.

Some thirty years later the first steel-framed skyscrapers
were built in America by a group of Chicago architects. In
the 1880s and 1890s this small group of architects — and
other individuals springing up in various European
countries — was part of an architectural trend that had been
at work throughout the century. A small underground

*One of the early American breakaways from the European
Renaissance tradition, the Schlesinger & Mayer department store
building (now Carson Pirie Scott & Co.) in Chicago, designed by
Louis Sullivan, introduced a new aesthetic using steel-frame
construction.*

stream of creativity, it had been flowing along, quietly
exploring new forms with new materials and new
technological advances. The group was flexible about developing a new aesthetic and, in some cases, pulling together the architects' realm and the engineers' territory
with simple, dignified, logical forms for utilitarian buildings.

In the matter of style, the eclecticism of the nineteenth
century continued into the twentieth century, but, over-all,

the greatest influence on the buildings of the twentieth century, and the most lasting, was a technical heritage: the use
of iron and steel, of glass; the discovery and production of
many new metals and their combinations known as alloys;
and the invention of the elevator, which made possible the
new skyscraper heights. All these changed not only the looks
of architecture but also the scale. It was never to be the same
again.

In the twentieth century the development of architectural
styles has emphasized different aspects of a general
"modern" concept. It has been a concept that moves and
changes at the same fast pace as the motors and designs of
our automobiles, occasionally, like them, getting snarled in
the traffic jams of controversy.

There are those today who remember the motor cars, not
yet called automobiles, of yesteryear. Their shapes and
performances were quite different from the cars on the
roads today, but they were nevertheless recognizably
automobiles, not carriages, and this is one way we might
think about different styles of "modern" buildings and
a changing skyline.

In style the skyscrapers of the early 1900s were multiwin-
dowed elongated eclectic buildings compared with the glass
checkerboard or glass-sheathed facades of the unadorned
later versions of *modern*. Skycrapers are commonly accepted as an American invention, but those earlier buildings, still nestled in among later models, can be seen to be
wearing distinctly foreign headdresses, topped off as they
invariably were by miniature Roman temples, Romanesque
towers, Gothic peaks and pinnacles, Italianate villas, and
high-sloped mansard-roofed Renaissance pavilions disguis-
ing their water towers. There was a time, before many of
these fanciful cover-ups fell into disrepair, when a course in
historical styles might have been conducted by helicopter;

*Modern technology, modern aesthetics, and modern life changed the skyline radically in the twentieth century and continues to reshape it.*

today those that are left make it easy to approximate a date before or after the 1930s for a skyscraper by looking at its top.

The style of the later skyscrapers and of many other contemporary buildings — the severe, unornamented use of metal and glass — had its beginnings in what later came to be called by art and architecture historians the International Style. The idea of clean-cut, functional form was at first a reaction against the *eclectic* and the teachings of the Beaux-Arts School of Architecture in France, which concentrated on principles developed during the Renaissance classic period. The movement toward this new functional approach had a slow beginning in Germany and Austria, where early in the twentieth century Austrian architect Adolf Loos wrote a famous line: "Ornament is crime." It was a statement without much popular appeal at the time, but following the devastation of World War I, when *social* and *economic* conditions in both Europe and America emphasized the need for minimal low-cost housing, the building of purely functional, unornamented, straight-line structures accelerated and the style spread throughout Europe and America undistinguished by national characteristics. Hence the name: *International*.

Two more twentieth-century statements promoted the strictly functional modern style. American architect Louis Sullivan, in his writings, stated that it was his belief that exterior form should faithfully follow function. This was translated into a stricter, more rigid admonition — "Form follows function" — and became the basic principle for a group of architects, including Walter Gropius and Mies van der Rohe of the *Bauhaus*, a German school of art. (Both these architects in later flight from the Hitler regime came to work and teach in the United States and profoundly affected United States architecture.) Mies van der Rohe pruned the last leaves from the vine of decoration with a final brief but enormously influential line, "Less is more."

One can understand and perhaps sympathize to a certain extent with the Modernists' intentions. Disturbed by the social chaos and physical rubble left by World War I, they envisioned an architecture that would have clean white or glass facades. Prefabricated, it would be cheap to build, and the world's unhappy homeless would be well housed. They seemed to believe that people the world over are alike and thus would be comfortable in the same housing and buildings. Modernism was a philosophy that tried to impose perfect design on an imperfect world . . . .*

And it has not always worked. Many people found the spaces too impersonal, the forms too unrelievedly rigid and cold. Nevertheless, it is still often resorted to in those places of the world where there is a need for fast, simple, economical building.

The International Style was a root style. It broke with the past, but it, too, has had its different periods, and even some of its most ardent early practitioners have moved away somewhat from its unrelenting severity, though not nearly so far afield as those in a contemporary rebellion that some critics now call *post-modern*, exemplified by an irreverent witticism which claims, "Less is a bore." This remark, too, will no doubt have its challengers ready to quip, "More is a mess," and so the controversies grow.

New and original uses of poured reinforced and precast concrete have been another modern trend resulting in structures in which the design ideal has been expressed in a combination of interesting as well as functional forms. Reinforced concrete is concrete slabs strengthened with steel reinforcing rods, and precast concrete is concrete

*Manuela Hoelterhoff in *The Wall Street Journal*, March 3, 1978.

poured into molds away from the construction site, the forms later moved into place. Both these techniques make possible many different curved, rounded, and molded shapes, as well as straight walls and supports. Effective sculptured buildings containing large-scale spaces sometimes have been the happy modern results of the use of concrete in this way, and its practical applications have included improved designs of highway dividers, ramps, and large parking garages.

A third trend which paralleled the International Style in time has been the influence of American architect Frank Lloyd Wright, important not only in his own country but throughout Europe. Wright's work and ideas were especially appreciated in Holland, where the Dutch were of the first to publish his writings and where numerous buildings show his principles to have been well understood there. Wright's originality and his view of building design as an organic whole, a total functioning unit related to nature, broke the mold of the traditional Victorian house. His characteristic long, low, horizontal lines in his designs for houses and the simplicity and uncluttered flow of spaces in all his buildings were a modern breakaway from the past.

Wright's early training was in engineering. At the end of the nineteenth century, when he attended the University of Wisconsin, there was not yet a school of architecture there. He was, therefore, one of the modernists who put *technology* to work *in accordance with nature* to provide aesthetically satisfying and sometimes very beautiful spaces for modern ways of living.

Another modern trend has been the development of the architectural team. This concept is a characteristic of the twentieth century not only in architecture, but in politics, corporate business, and medicine as well. On the architectural team, the architect remains primarily the artist-designer and organizer but works with specialists, who may be mechanical or structural engineers or experts on wind and anti-earthquake problems, on fire protection, on acoustics, on legal allowances and restrictions, and the many other complex technical problems involved even before actual construction teams come into the picture. It will never be possible again, for example, to duplicate exactly the acoustics of the Greek outdoor theater built on a chosen resonant hillside, or the original sound of a Renaissance opera house, for in the twentieth century techniques must be found to isolate the noise of air and road traffic, the underground rumblings of subways, and the sounds of air conditioning in auditoriums. All these factors have become an intrinsic part of city space, surrounding and influencing a building on any modern site.

Will the teams of the future be the same as those of today? Probably not. They may have to include outer-space ex-

*Frank Lloyd Wright was an original. In his houses, using modern materials and techniques, and, in general, simple horizontal planes, he was able to achieve an uncommon warmth and grace.*

perts, undersea construction specialists, and motion engineers, to mention only a few possibilities.

We go out of our twentieth-century houses into the streets of a twentieth-century city, or we drive our twentieth-century automobile along a highway to a twentieth-century shopping center in a twentieth-century town. We are moving through spaces we ourselves have affected and continue to influence by our ways of living, by our political and religious beliefs and our individual values. Armed with our knowledge of influences, what do we see?

Can we understand why certain buildings and their details are the way they are? What statements do they make? What do they indicate about our society, good or bad? How close has the architect come to giving us forms that are satisfying, exciting, or interesting and yet part of today? What has been inherited from the past? What in our society may have stimulated or discouraged and limited the beautiful?

Each individual will have a personal opinion, a personal bias, a personal nostalgia, a personal criticism. Some will see in huge glass skyscrapers an open, equalizing, democratic society; others will find them symbols of materialism, overwhelming the once-important religious buildings. They will liken them to the corporate image, or see in them only the powerful economic influence of speculative real estate development. The technical-minded will delight in fantastic structural solutions and the wide use and availability of all kinds of materials. Some will see dynamic movement combined with expert mechanical comfort; others will lament the hodgepodge of new and experimental materials and shapes and forms with little unity in relationship to the rest of the street; and still others will deplore the superefficiency of a machine-like technocracy. It is a combination of such personal feelings and the ways they react with the feelings and actions of others that gives society its answers.

It is obvious that except for the role *people* play, *technology* and *economics* are the most important influences on almost all buildings today, just as they seem to be the strongest elements affecting modern society. In New York City we pass the blank, windowless facades of the AT&T Long Lines building which protects intricate electronic long-distance telephone transmission equipment, and as we walk on, we are aware that in many of the newer skyscrapers windows are fixed and sealed against opening. Suddenly we realize that *climate* no longer has much to do with characterizing structures, since interior climate can be produced by choice. Will the window, then, eventually become chiefly a decorative element, with a history similar to that of the fireplace? Or will it change in form and shape to become once more useful and influential in a different role, as part, perhaps, of solar heating inventions developed to counteract energy shortages?

We walk through a newly built school and find what is called an open plan: spaces without walls; shelves of books or other furnishings functioning as movable divisions. Is this innovation in interior space due to new technology, or the whim of the architect, or are the spaces the result of new methods of teaching?

We see a security guard on duty in the lobby of an office building. How will our growing fears about security (*people*), emphasized by the widespread, almost immediate transmission of crime news by newspapers, radio, and TV (*technology*), affect the forms and spaces, the number and placement of exits, the width of stairways, the lighting and placement of windows, the elevators, the open court spaces, the use of balconies, the choice of sites of new buildings?

We pass an empty lot, a group of delapidated buildings, traces of their old character still noticeable, and we ponder the questions of renovation and restoration.

Time softens, makes mellow and familiar many buildings that once surprised or disturbed us because of their untraditional forms. But time, also, can be cruel and heartless. It makes obsolete some of our finest buildings and most beautiful landscapes. When this happens the question is: restore or replace? Although the question is usually posed as an aesthetic one, answers in our economic society are seldom based on aesthetics. They grow out of tax laws, fire laws, zoning regulations, construction union agreements (*people*), and out of *economics*. Unfortunately, restoration is often more expensive than replacement because the new is made up of predominantly standardized available materials. While the aesthetic arguments rage, the commercial, the opportunistic, and the economical move in with an irrefutable account sheet. They can be held at bay only by laws that encourage restoration and make it economically feasible (*people-political*). To restore purely out of nostalgia can be as arbitrary as tearing down just to replace with the new and urgent. The trouble with mixing nostalgia and architecture is that nostalgia is selective. No one really wants to return the serfs with the castle, or medieval plumbing with the cathedral, or royalty with Versailles, or even the old brownstone washtubs.

Over a period of time we watch the skyline and see a new super-scale developing. Skyscrapers no longer appear to be attempting to penetrate and explore space but to be swallowing it, devouring in one gulp a huge piece of sky. And yet, as a result of contemporary zoning laws (*people-political*), which insist on certain ground-level open areas in return for allowing greater height and volume on a city site, these same buildings have developed a number of interesting, exciting, well-proportioned, enjoyable arcades, shopping malls, and other pedestrian features. Is this to be the common future scale trade-off — massiveness above, community scale below? Is this the individual's or society's compromise with "big business"? And is it a good one?

What do these changing scales mean in terms of the individual of today? Is the individual important and vital only at the wheel of a machine, by the side of a computer, or encapsuled in a rocket? Are we being overwhelmed as human beings by economic systems and technology?

We are reminded that within the last forty years, humans and technology together have split an atom and put a man on the moon, and in doing so have given us a new world view of our universe as but one of an infinite number of universes. The previous great change in world view took place when Copernicus's theories showed the sun, rather than the earth, to be the center of a single universe of revolving planets. At that time the new view of the world, added to other scientific and geographic discoveries, created upheavals and transitional changes not only in beliefs but in patterns of living. The result was a culture more recognizably modern than societies of the past, in which there eventually flowered a series of artistic renaissances.

Could it be that we, too, are coming out of the dark ages of mechanization and industrialization, that individuals and societies as a whole are again in a major transitional period, on the way to new roles, to a new consciousness of their relationship and responsibility to each other? Perhaps with forethought, determination, and a little luck, we will reach new renaissances also. Perhaps we will find a new definition for progress. Perhaps we will learn how to control and direct new technological inventions, to plan and build in ways that link technology and ecology, improve the quality of living, and satisfy the human spirit.

# Bibliography

Anderson, William J. *The Architecture of the Renaissance in Italy*. London: B. T. Batsford, 1909.

Argan, Giulio C. *The Renaissance City*. New York: George Braziller, 1969.

Bacon, Edmund N. *Design of Cities*. New York: The Viking Press, 1967. Rev. ed. 1974.

Boyd, E. W. *English Cathedrals*. New York: Thomas Whittaker, 1884.

Branner, Robert *Gothic Architecture*. New York: George Braziller, 1961.

Brooks, Alfred M. *Architecture: Our Debt to Greece and Rome*. New York: Cooper Square Publishers, 1963.

*Buildings of Europe Series*. Ed. by Harald Busch and Bernd Lohse. *Romanesque Europe*. London: B. T. Batsford, Ltd, 1960. *Gothic Europe*. London: B. T. Batsford, Ltd, 1959.

Charpentrat, Pierre. *Living Architecture: Baroque*. New York: Grosset & Dunlap, Inc., 1967

Chermayeff, Sergius, and Alexander, Christopher. *Community and Privacy*. New York: Doubleday & Co., 1963. Pelican Books, 1966.

Clark, Kenneth. *Masterpieces of Fifty Centuries* (Introduction). New York: E. P. Dutton & Co., The Metropolitan Museum of Art, 1970.

Copplestone, Trewin, ed. *World Architecture*. (An Illustrated History.) New York: McGraw-Hill Book Co., N.D.

Couperie, Pierre. *Paris Through the Ages*. New York: George Braziller, 1971. Trans. from *Paris au fil du temps*. Cuénot, 1968.

Cronin, Vincent. *The Florentine Renaissance*. New York: E. P. Dutton & Co., 1967.

Cullen, Gordon. *Townscape*. London: The Architectural Press, 1961.

De Camp, L. Sprague. *The Ancient Engineers*. Garden City, N.Y.: Doubleday & Co., 1963.

193

De Cenival, Jean-Louis. *Living Árchitecture: Egyptian*. New York: Grosset & Dunlap, Inc., 1964.

de Wolfe. See Wolfe (de).

Flacelière, Robert. *Daily Life in Greece at the Time of Pericles*. Trans. Peter Green, from the French. New York: The Macmillan Co., 1965.

Fletcher, Sir Banister. *A History of Architecture*. Rev. ed. New York: Charles Scribner's Sons, 1963.

Foure, Helene. *The French Cathedrals: Their Symbolic Significance*. Boston: Bruce Humphries, Inc., 1931.

Gilmore, Myron P. *The World of Humanism 1453-1517*. New York: Harper Bros., 1952.

Gimpel, Jean. *The Cathedral Builders*. New York: Grove Press, Inc., 1961.

Hall, Edward Twitchell. *The Silent Language*. New York: Doubleday & Co., 1959.

Hamlin, Talbot. *Architecture Through the Ages*. Rev. ed. New York: G. P. Putnam's Sons, 1953.

Hamlin, Talbot, ed. *Forms and Functions of 20th Century Architecture, Vol. III*. New York: Columbia University Press, 1952.

Harris, Cyril M., ed. *Historic Architecture Source Book*. New York: McGraw-Hill Book Co., 1977.

Hofstatter, Hans H. *Living Architecture: Gothic*. New York: Grosset & Dunlap, Inc., 1970.

Jacquet, Pierre. *A History of Architecture*. The New Illustrated Library of Science and Invention, Leisure Arts, Ltd., London.

Jordan, R. Furneaux. *A Concise History of Western Architecture*. London: Thames and Hudson, 1969. New York: Harcourt Brace Jovanovich, Inc., 1970.

Lancaster, Osbert. *Sailing to Byzantium*. Boston: Gambit, Inc., 1969.

————. *Here, of All Places*. Boston: Houghton Mifflin Co., 1958.

Lowry, Bates. *Renaissance Architecture*. New York: George Braziller, 1971.

MacDonald, William. *Early Christian and Byzantine Architecture*. New York: George Braziller, 1962.

Mansbridge, John. *Graphic History of Architecture*. New York: The Viking Press, 1967.

Martin, Roland. *Living Architecture: Greek*. New York: Grosset & Dunlap, Inc., 1967.

Mertz, Barbara. *Red Land, Black Land: The World of the Ancient Egyptians*. New York: Coward-McCann, Inc., 1966.

Moholy-Nagy, Sibyl. *Native Genius in Anonymous Architecture*. New York: Horizon Press, Inc., 1957.

Mumford, Lewis. *Sticks and Stones*. New York: Dover Publications, Inc., 1955.

Norwich, John Julius, ed. *Great Architecture of the World*. New York: Random House and American Heritage Publishing Co., 1975.

Oursel, Raymond. *Living Architecture: Romanesque*. New York: Grosset & Dunlap, Inc., 1967.

Palladio, Andrea. *The Four Books of Architecture*. New York: Dover Publications, Inc., 1965.

Picard, Gilbert. *Living Architecture: Roman*. New York: Grosset & Dunlap, Inc., 1965.

Pollio, Marcus Vitruvius. *The Ten Books on Architecture*. Trans. M. H. Morgan. New York: Dover Publications, Inc., 1960.

Read, Herbert. *The Grass Roots of Art*. New York: Wittenborn, Schultz, Inc., 1949.

Robertson, D. S. *A Handbook of Greek and Roman Architecture*. Cambridge, Mass.: Cambridge University Press, 1943.

Rodin, Auguste. *Cathedrals of France*. Trans. Elisabeth Geiss-buhler. Boston: Beacon Press, 1965.

Rowland, Kurt. *The Shape of Towns*. London: Ginn and Company, Ltd., 1966.

Rudofsky, Bernard. *The Prodigious Builders*. New York and London: Harcourt Brace Jovanovich, 1977.

————. *Streets for People*. New York: Doubleday & Co., Inc., 1969.

Schneider, Wolf. *Babylon Is Everywhere: The City as Man's Fate*. New York: McGraw-Hill Book Co., 1963.

Scranton, Robert L. *Greek Architecture*. Braziller Series. New York: George Braziller, 1962.

Singleton, Esther. *Turrets, Towers, and Temples*. New York: Dodd, Mead & Co., 1898.

Smith, T. Roger. *Architecture: Gothic and Renaissance*. New York: Scribner and Welford, 1880. London: Sampson, Low, Marston, Searle & Rivington, 1880.

Spreiregen, Paul D. *The Architecture of Towns and Cities*. New York: McGraw-Hill Book Co., 1965.

Thiry, Paul; Bennett, Richard M.; Kamphoefner, Henry L. *Churches and Temples*. New York: Reinhold Publishing Corp., 1953.

Vasari, Giorgio. *Lives of the Artists*. Trans. George Bull. Baltimore: Penguin Books, 1965. Rev. ed. 1971.

Vitruvius. See Pollio.

Watterson, Joseph. *Architecture: A Short History*. Rev. ed. New York: W. W. Norton & Co., Inc., 1968.

Wolfe, de, Ivor. *The Italian Townscape*. New York: George Braziller, 1966.

Wright, Frank Lloyd. *Writings and Buildings*. Selected by Kaufmann, Edgar; and Raeburn, Ben. New York: Meridian Books, Inc. 1960.

Wycherly, R. E. *How the Greeks Built Cities*. New York: The Macmillan Co., 1949.

Zevi, Bruno. *Architecture as Space*. New York; Horizon Press, 1957.

Zucker, Paul. *Town and Square*. New York: Columbia University Press, 1959.

# Index

197

# About the Author

Anita Abramovitz received her B.A. degree from Sarah Lawrence College. She has been an editorial assistant at *The New Yorker* magazine and a teacher of remedial reading. Mrs. Abramovitz and her well-known architect husband, Max, have traveled extensively in Europe and have spent much time in Paris and its environs, where he has designed three buildings. Mrs. Abramovitz and her husband live in New York City.

# About the Illustrator

Susannah Kelly, originally from San Francisco, is a resident of New York City. She received her B.F.A. from The Cooper Union for the Advancement of Science and Art. As a free-lancer, she has done illustrations for RCA records, London Records, and *The New York Times*.